TUCKER'S COUNTRYSIDE

George Selden

ILLUSTRATED BY

Garth Williams

 CAMELOT BOOKS/PUBLISHED BY AVON

AVON BOOKS
A division of
The Hearst Corporation
959 Eighth Avenue
New York, New York 10019

Text copyright © 1969 by George Selden Thompson
Pictures copyright © 1969 by Garth Williams
Published by arrangement with Farrar, Straus & Giroux, Inc.
Library of Congress Catalog Card Number: 69-14975

ISBN: 0-380-01584-6

First Camelot Printing, February, 1972
Eighth Printing

CAMELOT TRADEMARK REG. U.S. PAT. OFF. AND
FOREIGN COUNTRIES, REGISTERED TRADEMARK—
MARCA REGISTRADA, HECHO EN U.S.A.

Printed in the U.S.A.

Map of Tucker's Countryside
by Tucker & Ellen. 1969

CAMELOT GEORGE SELDEN, born in Connecticut, now lives in New York. He has written many books for children, including the Newbery Award winning THE CRICKET IN TIMES SQUARE.

CONTENTS

For Don Reynolds,
with thanks for being who he is

TUCKER'S COUNTRYSIDE

ONE

John Robin

Tucker Mouse was definitely suffering from a touch of spring fever.

It happened every year toward the end of May. The course of the sun swung over just far enough, and a single bright ray was able to dart down through a grating in the sidewalk of Times Square, make its way through a maze of pipes and pillars in the subway station, and land, with a golden splash, right in front of the drain pipe where Tucker lived. Of course, in a week or so the sun would move on, and that ray would have to waste itself up in the streets of New York. But for these few days Tucker Mouse had sunshine on his doorstep—which is something very hard to have, if you live in the subway station at Times Square!

And he had something even more wonderful, too. Warmed by the sun, a few blades of grass were sprouting out of a pile of dirt right next to the drain pipe. Tucker didn't have any idea how the seeds could have gotten down there in the first place. But there they were—three lovely green blades, poking up through all the soot and dust. Tucker called them his "garden" and watered them twice a day with whatever he could collect in a paper cup from a leaky pipe in the subway walls. They wouldn't last long either. Even before the sun had moved on, he knew that the grass would be trampled down by all the commuters who streamed through the subway station every morning and evening. It made him sort of sad, to think that his grass would soon be gone.

But today, at least, he had his garden and a puddle of sunlight to sit in as well. And the air was sweet and soft and clean, the way the air gets in the springtime— even in the Times Square subway station—and Tucker Mouse really did have a very bad case of spring fever. It was getting worse by the minute. He had decided to go back inside the drain pipe and take a nap before he fell asleep right there, out in the open, and got himself stepped on, when something caught his eye.

It was a flutter of little wings behind the Bellinis' newsstand. Tucker peered more closely. Then he called back into the drain pipe, "Harry, there's a bird in the subway station."

A few feet within the wall the pipe opened out into a larger space, where Tucker kept all the things he'd collected. Harry Cat was lying back there, stretched out on a pile of crumpled newspapers, half asleep and half awake to the lovely afternoon. "Is it a pigeon?" he asked. Sometimes a pigeon would fly into the station

4

and flutter around for days before it found its way out again.

"No," said Tucker. "It's a little bird."

Harry padded softly to the opening of the drain pipe and stuck his head out where Tucker was sitting. "Where?"

"Over there," said Tucker. "He's sitting on top of the Bellinis' newsstand."

Harry Cat studied the bird a minute. "It's a robin," he said. "See the red on his chest? Now what would a robin be doing down here?"

"Maybe he's going to take the shuttle over to Grand Central Station," said Tucker.

"Don't be silly!" said Harry Cat. "He'd fly."

Just then the robin flickered up from the back of the newsstand and began to fly around the station. He perched for a second on the roof of one of the shuttle cars—then swooped over toward the Nedick's lunch counter.

"I think he's looking for something," said Harry.

And indeed the robin was looking for something. He whished past the lunch counter and gave Mickey, the counterman, such a start that he let a chocolate soda overflow. Then the little bird darted over toward the Loft's Candy Store, brushed past its glass windows, circled back over the opening to the drain pipe, and suddenly—much to Tucker's and Harry's surprise—dropped down and landed right in front of them.

"Whee-*ooo!*" said the robin. "Thought I'd never find you." He hopped up close to the opening and then hopped back again. "You *are* Tucker Mouse, aren't you?"

"Yes," said Tucker. "Who are you?"

"John Robin," said the little bird. He took a few more hops, back and forth. "And this would be—um—"

"Harry Cat," said Harry.

"Yes, well, I—uh—" John Robin couldn't seem to stand still. He would hop up, almost inside the drain pipe, and then quickly jump away again.

"What are you bouncing around like that for?" said Tucker Mouse.

"Well, it's just that I—uh—I mean, he really *is* a—a sort of a *cat,* you know. And up in Connecticut, where I come from, birds and cats don't—it's awfully old-fashioned, I guess—but they just don't get along to well."

"Harry, he's scared of you," said Tucker. "Do something nice to show him it's all right."

Harry Cat grinned and said, "What shall I do? Purr a little? Mmmmmmm!" He gave out a long, contented cat's purr.

"Just don't eat me!" said John Robin. "That'll be nice enough. Chester said he was sure you wouldn't, but—"

"Chester *Cricket?*" burst out Tucker. "Do you know Chester?"

"Course I know him," said the robin. "Known him for years. Dorothy and I—she's my wife—we nest in the willow tree next to his stump."

"How is he?" said Harry, purring in earnest now because he was so happy to hear some news of his old friend.

"Oh, he's fine," said John Robin. "Chipper as ever."

"Does he still play as beautifully as he used to?" asked Tucker.

"Even more so."

"What a musician!" Tucker shook his head in wonderment. "Did he tell you about what happened to him down here in New York?"

"Oh yes," said John Robin. "When he got back last September, he told us all about it. Very nice, I'm sure. But you know, we've got a *lot* of good musicians up in the Meadow." The little bird cocked his head rather proudly to one side. "Far as that goes, I'm not a half-bad singer myself! But there's no time to talk about that now. I'm here on serious business."

"Come in the house," said Tucker. "It's almost time for the commuters, and I wouldn't want any friend of Chester's to get trampled on."

The cat and the mouse turned and went into the drain pipe, and John Robin, after one dubious look at the dark opening, hopped in after them. They all went up to the pocket inside and made themselves comfortable on the newspapers.

John Robin

"Now what's the serious business?" said Harry Cat.

"We've got big worries up in the Old Meadow," said John Robin. "Chester and Simon Turtle are just worried to death. They're sort of the heads of the Meadow—Simon because he's the oldest person there, and Chester, well, just because he's Chester—and they're almost frantic. We all are!"

"What's the problem?" asked Tucker.

"I'd rather wait and let Chester explain it to you himself," said the robin. "The point is, I was sent down to New York to ask you—in fact to *beg* you and Mister Cat here—"

"Call me Harry," said Harry.

"—to beg you and Harry to come up to Connecticut right away! Chester said that you used to be his manager and that you were very good at solving problems." The robin shook his head hopelessly. "And I'm here to tell you, we've sure got a problem up in the Old Meadow!"

Tucker looked at Harry and then looked back at John Robin. "Well, I don't know," he began. "Harry and I have talked about going to see Chester some time, but Connecticut's an awful long way away, and—"

"Oh, *please!*" interrupted the robin. "Connecticut's not so far. And if a little cricket like Chester could take the train up there, two big fellows like you certainly can too! We need you terribly! Honest! If

9

you don't come, I don't know *what* we're going to do!" John Robin was so upset and anxious that he hopped around frantically and got his claws all tangled up in torn newspapers. But he quieted down after a while and just stood staring at the floor of the drain pipe.

For a minute or so everyone was silent. Nobody looked at anybody. Then Harry Cat said quietly, "We'll go."

Tucker Mouse shrugged. "So—we'll go."

"Thank *goodness!*" The robin was so relieved that he burst out in a little, spontaneous song.

"When shall we leave?" said Harry.

"Could you come tonight?" John began bobbing up and down impatiently. "We could take the Late Local Express, the way Chester did."

"Tonight?" Tucker Mouse jumped up on his feet. "But I have to pack!"

"What do you have to pack?" said Harry Cat quizzically.

"Why, why—*everything!*" announced the mouse.

"Everything?" Harry looked around the drain pipe skeptically. Tucker's possessions were piled all over— in corners, on top of newspapers, under newspapers, everywhere.

"Of course!" said Tucker. He dashed over to one corner, picked up the heel of a lady's high-heel shoe, and cradled it gently in his arms. "You don't think I'd leave this beautiful heel here, do you?" He dropped the heel and dashed over to another corner. Shreds of newspaper flew up in a gale as he rummaged amid the mess. Then he held up two tiny white pearls. "And my pearls! *Surely,* Harry, you remember who it was who dashed out last January, when that lady's strand snapped, and salvaged these beautiful pearls!"

"It slips my mind," said Harry innocently.

"It was *me!*" said Tucker. "And right during rush hour too!"

"Well, they're only fake pearls," said Harry.

"Fake or not, they're *mine!*" shouted the mouse. "You know, Harry, you and me aren't the only people living in this subway station. There's a pack of dishonest rats living in the drain pipes on the other side, and they would *love* the chance to swipe a few of my things!" Another thought struck him; he dropped the pearls and clutched at his heart. "Oh, my buttons! My beautiful collection of buttons!"

"Now quiet down," said Harry Cat. As Tucker was dashing off to find his buttons, the big cat lifted his right front paw and brought it down on the mouse's back, squashing him—very gently—to the floor. That was how he helped his friend relax when Tucker got too excited.

"Harry, if you wouldn't mind—the paw, please, Harry—if you wouldn't mind."

"Will you be reasonable?" said Harry.

"I'm always reasonable," said Tucker Mouse.

Harry lifted his paw, and Tucker stood up. "And besides my heel, my pearls, my buttons, and all the keys, hairpins, and everything else I've managed to scrounge up through the years, what about *this?*" Very grandly Tucker marched across the drain pipe and pulled aside a sheet of paper propped against the wall. There, neatly piled up, were two dollars and eighty-six cents, in pennies, nickels, dimes, and quarters, with one big half dollar on the bottom. "My life savings!" proclaimed Tucker Mouse. "And wouldn't those rats love to get their claws on this! Believe me, Harry, they wouldn't spend it on charity!"

"I'll take care of everything—once and for all!" said Harry Cat. Usually Harry moved in a slow, stealthy way, but sometimes he moved like lightning—as he did now. Before either Tucker or John Robin knew what was happening, the big cat began to sweep all Tucker's valuables into a heap.

Tucker was frantic when he saw what was happening. "Harry, stop! What are you doing? Oh—my buttons! Don't scratch the pearls! *My life savings—!*"

In a cascade of silver Harry pushed over the column of small change and added it to the mound of Tucker's possessions. Then, with one paw, he pulled away a little section of the drain-pipe wall and revealed a dark hole. As Tucker danced around madly, shouting, "It won't be safe! It won't be safe!" Harry scooped all the

things inside the tiny cave and replaced the section of wall. "There!" Harry said, when the work was finished. "And it *will* be safe!" He rubbed his fur back and forth against the spot where Tucker's treasure had disappeared. "I'll leave a lot of cat smell here. Any rat who noses around will get the daylights scared out of him!"

"Ruined!" Tucker Mouse wrung his two front paws. "I'm ruined. The fruits of all these years of scrounging —gone!"

"And they'll still be here when we get back," said Harry Cat. "Now how about something to eat? John must be hungry if he flew all the way down from Connecticut—aren't you, John?"

"I don't want to be any trouble," said the robin, who secretly was famished but didn't think he'd find anything he liked to eat in New York.

The thought of food made Tucker perk up a little. "What's your preference?" he asked the little bird.

"Oh—worms, mostly," said John.

"Worms I don't have," said Tucker. "And don't want."

"I also like seeds," said John Robin.

"Seeds. Hmmm." Tucker Mouse wiggled his whiskers—which helped him think. He went over to the part of the drain pipe he called "the pantry," where he kept all the bits of sandwiches and candy bars and other things he picked up around the lunch counters in the station. A minute's fumbling and he had found what he was looking for—a big crust, which he brought over and set down in front of the robin. "It's from a seeded roll," he said. "You could peck out the seeds."

John took a peck at the crust. "Delicious! Never tasted anything like it!"

"A mere poppyseed roll," said Tucker with a wave of his paw. "New York is full of such wonders."

"And after we eat I want to hear you sing some more," said Harry.

"Be glad to," said John Robin with a mouthful of poppy seeds.

About half an hour later a man named Anderson was passing through the subway station on his way home to New Rochelle. He heard something and stopped to listen. The sound stopped too. But then, in a moment, it started again. Mr. Anderson shook his head. He knew it was impossible, but it actually sounded like a little songbird—singing to his heart's delight inside that drain-pipe opening.

TWO

Connecticut

Late that night the cat, the mouse, and the robin were almost ready to leave for Connecticut. John Robin was hopping back and forth impatiently. "Don't you think we ought to get going?" he said. "We don't want to miss the train."

"Tucker, what are you doing?" called Harry Cat.

Tucker Mouse was over in his pantry, making a great stir about something. He came back to the others carrying a big package neatly wrapped in wax paper retrieved from the Nedick's lunch counter and tied with string from the Loft's Candy Store. "This is one thing I *am* taking," he said.

"What is it?" said Harry.

"Never mind." Tucker held the bundle out of the cat's reach. "It's something for Chester."

"Gee, let's *go!*" In his impatience John Robin hopped up so high that he hit his head on the drain-pipe ceiling.

Tucker's Countryside

"All right, all right," said Tucker. "Take it easy. I don't want you braining yourself in my living room." He sighed and took a last look around the drain pipe. "My nice home—I wonder if I'll ever see it again."

"Of course you will," said Harry Cat. "Now come on."

They began the climb up through the labyrinth of pipes to the street. Harry went first, Tucker last, and John Robin stayed in the middle so he wouldn't get lost down any of the dozens of openings they passed. In a few minutes they were on the sidewalk. Times Square stretched up above and all around them. Most of the moviegoers and crowds from the theaters had gone home, but the huge neon signs were still spilling their torrents of color over the Square.

"Goodbye, Times Square," said Tucker Mouse. "The soul who loves you most is going away."

"For goodness' sakes!" said Harry Cat. "You sound like the last act of an Italian opera!" Harry liked opera very much and had sneaked into the Metropolitan Opera House many times.

The three of them went down Forty-second Street toward Grand Central Station. John Robin flew on ahead—it was easier for him than hopping—and then waited on the curb until the cat and the mouse came creeping along under the cars that lined the street.

They reached Bryant Park, the neat little patch of grass and trees behind the Public Library on the corner of Fifth Avenue. "That's the only countryside I've ever seen," said Tucker to the robin.

John flew up, circled once over the park, and came back. "Why, that's nothing!" he said. "Most of the houses near the Meadow have *lawns* that are bigger than that!"

They continued on. While Harry and Tucker were padding silently under a big Cadillac, the mouse suddenly said, "Harry, if even the houses have lawns that are bigger than Bryant Park, there must be a lot of open space in Connecticut."

"I guess so," said Harry Cat.

"Do they have wild animals in Connecticut, Harry?"

"Most likely."

"What kind of wild animals?"

"Oh—lions, tigers. Elephants, maybe."

"Harry, if you wouldn't mind—be serious, please!"

"Don't worry, Mousiekins," said Harry. "I'll protect you!" He sometimes called Tucker "Mousiekins" when he wanted to tease him.

But Tucker was not amused. He trudged along behind, muttering, "Bears. I'll bet they have bears anyway."

And at last they reached Grand Central Station. Down they went, through the same series of pipes and deserted corridors and drafty back rooms that Tucker and Harry had passed last September. But then Chester Cricket had been clinging tightly to the fur on Harry's back. The Late Local Express was still leaving from track 18. This time of night there were very few passengers, so the animals had no trouble slipping into a shady corner in one of the compartments between the cars. And they didn't have long to wait either. In a few minutes there was a lurch and a screech of iron wheels, and the train began to move.

"We're going!" shouted Tucker Mouse. "I feel it—we're really moving, Harry! Our first trip anywhere! Oh! oh! oh!"

"Now, take it easy," said Harry Cat, and lifted his right front paw.

"You wouldn't squash me, please, Harry," said Tucker indignantly. "That's no way to begin a trip!"

"Then don't get too excited," said Harry, and lowered his paw.

"A fine thing!" sniffed Tucker Mouse. "I couldn't even get excited on my very first journey!"

"You can get excited, Mousiekins. But *not* hysterical!"

They all settled back to enjoy the ride.

Three and a half hours later the three friends were wondering about the name of the train they were on. They understood the "Late" and the "Local" part, but they couldn't imagine why anyone would call it an "Express." It seemed to stop at every crossroads, and when it did stop, it waited—and waited—and *waited!*

Connecticut

"We've been on this thing long enough to get to Canada!" complained Harry Cat. He was a very curious cat, Harry was, and he enjoyed looking at the maps that sometimes appeared in the newspapers he and Tucker used to furnish their home. So he knew the direction in which they were traveling: northwest and then due north.

"I think we're almost there," said John Robin. He flew up and took a look out of the window in the compartment where they were. In the black night heavens, the moon, which was just a few days past the full, was shining brightly. It looked as if some great sky monster had begun to nibble away at it. "I was right—we're here!" said John, and flew down again. "I recognize the houses outside."

"Thank goodness!" said Tucker Mouse. He stood up and stretched his limbs. They were sore from the pounding of the wheels below. "We should have stowed away on a Greyhound bus instead."

The train rattled to a halt. "Everybody off!" said the robin. Since no one was getting out at this station, the conductor didn't bother to open the door, and the animals had to scramble down through an opening between two cars. "Welcome to *Hedley!*" said John when they were on the platform.

"Is that the name of the town?" said Harry.

"Yes." The robin pointed with one wing. Down on the wall of the station house a sign lit up by an electric bulb said HEDLEY CONNECTICUT. "Hedley was the name of the man who settled this whole part of the state."

Tucker Mouse looked around. "Where's Chester?"

"Oh, it was too far for him to come all the way to the station," said John. "I'm afraid we have a long walk ahead of us."

"I don't care *how* long it is!" said Harry Cat. "As long as we're off that train!"

They set off, with John Robin sometimes fluttering, sometimes hopping along in the lead. Tucker had a hard time with his package. He tried to carry it first in his right front paw, then in his left front, then switching often from one to the other. It seemed to get heavier and heavier, and he kept falling farther and farther behind. He wouldn't think of abandoning it, though. When Harry saw what was happening, he went up to Tucker without a word and hooked the string around the package under one of his sharp lower teeth. It was no weight at all for a big cat like Harry.

They went on walking. At first they passed stores, offices, a movie theater—the kind of buildings you would find in the center of a town. There was almost no one on the streets. The store fronts were dark, and only the high street lights cast patches of brightness down where the animals scurried along. Then, when they got to the parts of Hedley where people lived, there were apartment houses, and two-family houses, and finally single-family homes. Tucker had never seen one before in his life, and even Harry had only seen the town houses of the upper East Side in New York, and they were all connected.

"I couldn't believe it!" said Tucker Mouse. "Look at the size of that lawn over there! John was right—it's bigger than Bryant Park!"

"I 'ike it here!" said Harry enthusiastically. "It's beau'i'ul in 'onne'i'uh—'onnekikuk—" He gave up trying to say "Connecticut" with Tucker's package dangling from his mouth.

And on they padded. Until, on their left, a vast darkness appeared. No houses or lawns were there. But the moon, which was dropping toward the morning, silvered the branches of trees and bushes. And a sound of running water came rustling up to them. "The meadow starts here," said John Robin. "Do you hear the brook?

"It looks more like a jungle to me!" said Tucker Mouse.

"This is one of the woodsy parts," said John. "The flat part, with grass and everything, is down at the other end. That's where Chester lives. Can you make it?"

"Of 'ourse!" said Harry. In a minute, though, he suddenly dropped the package and said, "Did you hear anything?"

"Like what?" said Tucker.

From the dark ahead came a single chirp. Then another. And another.

"It's Chester!" shouted Harry. He grabbed up the bundle and dashed on into the night. Tucker Mouse scuttled after him, and John Robin took off and flew over them both.

A fence ran beside the road. With each post that Harry went past, the chirps sounded nearer and nearer. They seemed to be coming from one certain post. Harry stopped in front of it. "Chester!" he called up. "Is that you?"

And down, in one jump, from the top of the fencepost came Chester Cricket. "Harry!" he said. "I'm so *glad* to see you!" The cat gave him such a big lick on the head that it knocked him right over.

"Watch it, Harry," said Tucker Mouse, who came puffing up just then. "With a kiss like that, you could knock the cricket unconscious."

"Tucker!" exclaimed Chester Cricket. "Oh, isn't that wonderful!"

Then, naturally, everybody started hugging everybody. It isn't so easy to hug a cricket, either. And they all talked at once—exclaiming and laughing the way old friends do when they haven't seen each other for months and months.

"I've been waiting on that fencepost for hours!" said Chester.

"We've been *traveling* for hours!" said John Robin.

For no good reason everyone burst out laughing again. But gradually the laughter subsided into a few final chuckles. The robin began hopping around nervously. "I guess I'd better get back to my nest, Chester," he said. "It's almost light, and I'd like to get a little sleep at least. I have a big morning of worming planned for tomorrow."

"All right, John," said Chester. "And thanks for showing Tucker and Harry the way."

The cat and the mouse thanked him, too. Then the little bird flew off into the night. As he disappeared, they heard him saying, "Whee-*ooo!* Down to New York and back in one day! What a flight!"

"Come on," said Chester to Harry and Tucker. "I'll show you the way to my stump."

He led them under the lowest wire of the fence and out into the Old Meadow. There was a path worn through the grass, and the moon, although it was riding low on the horizon, still shed enough light for them to see where they were going. "Be careful you don't go too far off to the right," said Chester. "The bank drops right down to the brook. Can you both swim, by the way?"

"I can, but I hate it," said Harry Cat.

"I don't know if I can or not," said Tucker. "And I don't want to find out tonight." He moved a little over to the left.

Even before they reached his home, Chester insisted

on hearing all about New York—and especially the Bellini family. So, as they walked, and Chester hopped, Harry and Tucker told him the news. Mario was studying violin at the Juilliard School of Music. He had become so interested in music during Chester's stay in New York that he had decided to make it his career. "And I heard him tell Mr. Smedley that he chose the violin because it sounded more like a cricket's chirp than any other instrument," said Harry. As for Mr. Smedley, whose letter to *The New York Times* had launched Chester on his famous career, he had become one of the most successful piano teachers in the city. "Mostly because he keeps telling everybody that he was the one who discovered you," said Tucker. "And it was really me!" And Mama and Papa Bellini were doing very well, too. Most of the people who began coming to the newsstand while Chester was giving his concerts there kept buying their papers and magazines from the Bellinis even after the cricket had left. "And you know what," said Harry Cat. "After all those years of complaining about how old and rickety the newsstand was, when they *could* afford to have a new one made—they decided they didn't want to! Mama said it was too much like an old friend to have it changed. So there it stands—the same as always!"

"I'm glad," said Chester. "I like to think of everything just the way it was."

Their walk through the meadow had brought them

at last to Chester's stump. "This is just the way I imagined it," said Tucker Mouse. It was on a bank, not too high, not too low, just at the point where the brook made a turn. So it had the water bubbling on two sides. And a big willow tree dropped lacy branches over it.

"I hope there's room enough for Harry inside," said Chester as he hopped through an opening into the stump. "I had some field mice gnaw out some more space this afternoon."

"You have *mice* here?" said Tucker, following Chester in.

"Lots of them," said the cricket. "You'll meet everybody tomorrow."

"Plenty of room," said Harry. He stretched out on the spongy wooden floor of the stump.

Chester pointed at something above their heads. "Do you recognize that?" The moonlight, reflected from the brook, picked out a spark of silver.

"It's your bell!" said Tucker.

"My bell." The cricket nodded. "I found some string beside the road and tied it to the ceiling."

"Well, I have something else to remind you of New York," said the mouse. He began carefully untying the package, which he had carried himself since they left the road.

"At last we see what it is!" said Harry. "We've lugged that thing all the way from Times Square."

Connecticut

"Liverwurst!" exclaimed Chester. For Tucker Mouse had undone the wax paper to reveal a big chunk of the meat.

"Stolen only this morning from the Nedick's lunch counter," said Tucker. "Remember your first night in the city, when we had the liverwurst together? I thought it would be nice again."

"Oh, that *is* nice of you!" said Chester. "I haven't had any since I left New York."

So the three friends sat down to a delicious, late-night snack of liverwurst. And they talked and reminisced about Chester's adventures in the city, as always happens when old friends meet. And outside the tree stump the night wore away.

A lull came in the conversation, and Harry Cat said, "Now what's this big problem about the meadow, Chester?"

The cricket shook his head. "It's something very serious. Come on—I'll show you. It's almost sunrise—you'll be able to see." He jumped out the opening in the stump, then up on top of it. Harry and Tucker scrambled after him. Above them, a pale lavender light, the color of lilacs, seemed to lift the sky upwards. The heavens stood high. "Now look all around," said Chester, "all around the meadow, and tell me what you see."

Tucker and Harry did as they were told. They could see the flat, grassy land around Chester's stump, and farther off the woodsy part where the meadow began, and still farther, toward the west, a ridge of hills that were also covered with trees. Here and there, through the brush, through the reeds, they caught a glitter of the brook in its course. In the dawn the meadow looked so fresh, and everything in it, that it seemed as if it had just been created today.

"Beautiful!" said Harry Cat.

"But look *outside* the meadow!" said Chester. "Look all around outside."

Everywhere, on all sides—beyond the hills, beyond the woodsy parts—there were houses. To the east, where the sun was just coming up, two new ones were being built. "I only see houses," said Harry Cat.

"That's just it," said Chester. "Houses!"

Tucker Mouse scratched his head. "I don't get it, Chester. What's wrong with houses?"

"It's too long to go into now," said the cricket. "I'll explain it when we wake up. Let's get some sleep while we can."

THREE

The Old Meadow

None of the animals could sleep very well. Tucker and Harry were too excited at being up in Connecticut at last. And Chester Cricket, overjoyed as he was to see his friends again, was too worried about the Old Meadow to do anything but doze awhile. So after a few hours of napping they all decided it was silly to pretend to sleep when you weren't really sleeping, and got up.

The first thing they did was go down to the brook for a drink. *"Delicious!"* exclaimed Harry Cat as he tasted the icy, bubbling water. "It's certainly fresher than that stuff we collect from the pipes in the subway walls."

"Yes, but how many flavors does this brook come in?" said Tucker Mouse, who was thinking of all the soda pop he scrounged from the lunch counters in the station.

"Nothing tastes as good as my brook," said Chester Cricket. With his two front legs he sloshed a little cold water in his face. It was his habit to do that first thing every morning, even on the coldest days in winter, to wake himself up. "Let's go up on the stump again," he said. "You can see what the meadow looks like in broad daylight."

The cricket jumped up in one hop, and Tucker and Harry followed him. All around them the bright June morning sparkled on young leaves and blossoms newly opened. For a mouse whose only garden up till then had been three pathetic blades of grass, it was an overwhelming sight. Tucker felt his heart grow large with poetry. "Look how lovely, Harry!" he said. "Trees, flowers, little green growing things—ha-*choo!*" He gave a huge sneeze.

"God bless you," said Harry Cat.

"Thank you, Harry," said Tucker, and launched into a hymn in praise of Nature. "Oh, the countryside, the countryside!—ha-*choo!*" But it was interrupted by another sneeze, even larger than the first.

"What's the matter with you?" said Harry.

Tucker wiped his nose on one front paw—not a very nice thing to do, but he had no newspapers handy. Then he rubbed his eyes, which he suddenly realized had begun to itch. "Harry," he said gloomily, "I think I have hay fever."

"Don't tell me you're allergic to all those lovely little green growing things!" said Harry Cat slyly.

"You wouldn't rub it in, please, Harry," said the mouse. "Chester, do you have a newspaper or a Kleen-

ex or something in the stump? I have to blow my nose."

"I'm sorry, but I don't," said Chester Cricket.

"Then I'll have to use a leaf," said Tucker. He climbed down from the stump.

"Watch out you don't use poison ivy!" Harry Cat called after him.

Tucker searched along the bank of the brook and finally found a clump of fern. They were nice and soft, like Kleenex, but weren't really ideal for blowing the nose because they were very lacy and full of holes. Still, Tucker thought they were the best he could find. He picked a few extras and went back to the stump.

"Here's our nature lover—back from the fields and the glens!" said Harry Cat when Tucker sat sniffling beside him and Chester again.

Tucker blew his nose on a fern and then threw it in the brook. "I may be the only mouse in the world who has to use ferns as handkerchiefs," he said.

Harry Cat turned to Chester. "Now explain about the houses. Why do they worry you so much?"

Chester Cricket shook his head. "There's just too *many* of them! That's the whole problem. When I got back to Connecticut last fall, I found they'd built two new ones just in the time I was gone—down on the south side there. And this spring they've started *three* others. Besides those two in the east, across the road, there's one going up near the north corner of the meadow. All the animals who live here in the Old

Meadow are just scared to death that in a year or so there won't *be* any Old Meadow at all! Up till now the brook has saved us. It's marshy along the banks, and sometimes there's a little flooding. But just two weeks ago Bill Squirrel—he's a squirrel you'll meet later on; he's always swinging around in the trees near the houses, bringing back news—Bill said that he heard two homeowners talking about some plan the town of Hedley had to put the brook down in a conduit!"

"What's a conduit?" asked Tucker Mouse.

"It's like a big concrete pipe," said Chester. "And the plan is to put the brook down in this pipe and make it run through concrete underground instead of up in the open where it belongs. Then they could drain the marshy parts. And if they do that, there won't be any stopping them. They'll put up houses everywhere!"

"Wonderful!" said Tucker. "It'll be just like New York! Maybe they'll even build a subway!"

"But we don't *want* it to be like New York!" said Chester. "Now don't misunderstand. I love New York, and I had a wonderful time when I was living there. But I love the country even more. I don't have anything against houses either—if they stay where they should! Why, sometimes I even hop over just to be where the human beings live. I especially like the time around noon on a weekday. You can hear the housewives using the vacuum cleaner, or see them hanging the laundry up. And the dogs are snoozing in the sun on the doorsteps, waiting for kids to come home from school. I don't know—it makes me feel all funny and happy. Everything is so busy, but peaceful too. Then I'll hop back into the meadow—and I'm even happier here. Because this is *my* home!" The cricket took a long look around the meadow. In his eyes there was both love and ownership. Harry and Tucker glanced at each other.

"And it isn't just me," Chester went on. "What's going to happen to everyone else who lives here? I could get by in any little old bush, houses or no houses. And so could John Robin and Bill Squirrel; they don't mind houses, as long as there are trees around. But what about all the rabbits and the chipmunks and the pheasants? And Simon Turtle—it'll be the death of him if they put the brook underground!" The cricket fell silent and shifted uneasily from one set of legs to another. Tucker and Harry had never seen such a fretful look on his face.

"Now don't worry," said Harry Cat. "We'll think of something, Chester."

"I certainly hope so!" said Chester. "All the meadow folks I know—we haven't been able to come up with a single good idea!"

In order that the cat and the mouse might have a clear picture of the problem, and also to meet some of Chester's friends, the cricket took them both on a tour of the Old Meadow. It was roughly in the shape of a square. The brook, which started out life as the overflow of a reservoir, entered the meadow from the west at the southwest corner. It bubbled along parallel to the southern border until it came to the hilly, woody land in the southeast. There, since its way was blocked, it turned back toward the center of the meadow and proceeded northward. But then, for no apparent reason, when the brook was approaching the northern border, it suddenly changed its mind. It made a sharp turn—that was where Chester's stump was located—and flowed along in an eastern direction until it left the meadow at the northeast corner. It was as if the brook, like everyone else who lived in the Old Meadow, just simply loved the place and wanted to spend as much of its time as it could right there.

Chester first led his friends through what he called "Tuffet Country." That was the stretch of land just south of his stump. And, naturally, it was full of tuffets. It was also full of various rabbits and sundry fieldmice. That was how Chester introduced them. "There are too many of you to call by name," he said, "so I'll just say, Harry Cat and Tucker Mouse, these are various rabbits and sundry fieldmice."

Lots of timid little whiskered faces and soft brown rabbit eyes peeked out from around tuffets and through the tall grass. "I think the sundries are afraid of Harry," said Tucker Mouse under his breath.

"Nobody be scared!" said Chester in a loud voice. "These are friends. They've come to help us."

There was a rustling, whispery pause. Then a tiny voice, which probably came from the littlest sundry, shouted out, *"Hooray!"*

The three friends continued on through the meadow, walking beside the brook and stopping every now and again so that Tucker could pick a few more fern handkerchiefs. "Everybody is really counting on us, aren't they, Chester?" said the mouse. "To save the meadow, I mean."

"We certainly are!" said Chester. "We've been racking our brains for weeks and weeks, and not even Simon Turtle could think of anything."

"When do we meet Mr. Turtle?" said Harry Cat.

"Very soon now," answered Chester. "First we go through Pasture Land, and then we come to the pool where Simon lives. You know, the whole meadow used to be part of a farm. The farm house either burned down or fell down ages ago—the cellar is way over there in the west, across the brook, where those trees are—but the part where we are now, Pasture Land, is where the farmer kept his cows. See how nice and flat and green it is?"

And, indeed, the grass over which they walked now was as soft and thick as a tended lawn. Buttercups and forget-me-nots swarmed over the earth. And near the brook, where the soil was moist, tall irises lifted elegant purple blossoms. Tucker Mouse heaved a sigh. "Ah, the countryside!" Then he sneezed and blew his nose again.

At the end of Pasture Land they came to the hilly country where the brook turned in toward the center of the meadow. Beneath one of the rises the water had formed a deep, still pool. The current ran slow, and a glint of fish could be seen from the dark but living depths. This was Simon's Pool. And despite the fish who lived there, two or three crafty water snakes, and half a dozen pompous bullfrogs, there was no question who ruled the water. Simon Turtle was by far the oldest and also one of the most revered dwellers in the Old Meadow—even if he did have a tendency, like many old souls, to reminisce a little too much.

Chester found him taking the sun on the back of a big log that had floated up beside the bank. "Mr. Turtle, these are my friends Harry Cat and Tucker Mouse —the ones I told you about."

Simon craned his head out from under his black, wavy shell. His eyes were sharp and wise, but not unkind. He gave Harry and Tucker a long, hard look. And when those eyes had looked at you, you *knew* you'd been looked at! "Pleased to meet you," said Simon in a raspy, soft voice. Harry and Tucker both said they were glad to meet him, too. "What do you think of our meadow?" the turtle went on.

"Wonderful!" said Harry.

Tucker's Countryside

"Beautiful!" said Tucker, suppressing a sneeze.

"You should have seen it the way it was when I was your age," said Simon Turtle. "Now that was *real* country then! There were only three or four houses across the road there, in the east—and north and south, maybe one or two—and off west, none at all! Just good thick forested hills. Did you know there even used to be *deer* in the meadow?"

Chester Cricket could see that the old turtle was longing to share some of his recollections with Tucker and Harry. So he thought he'd just help him out with a hint. "One of Mr. Turtle's best friends was a deer named Ned."

"*The* best, Chester—*the* best," said Simon, "until I met you. What a buck he was too, Ned Deer! So strong and handsome, with beautiful tall antlers. And for some reason we just hit it off together and got to be best friends. I'm not very good at walking, you know— but when Ned and I would go for a stroll, he'd lounge along beside me on those long legs of his, very steady and slow, so that I could keep up. My, what talks we had! And what days!" The turtle shook his head at the joy the memory brought back to him. "But Ned's relations—they all used to live down here, too—and they knew what was happening. They could see what was written in the trees chopped down and the hills dug up. They told Ned they'd have to leave pretty soon—go out there west, beyond the reservoir, where it still was forested and good. And one by one they *did* leave. But not Ned. He stayed in the meadow—out of friendship for me, I think. Until finally he was the last deer left."

Simon Turtle's eyes went dark, and he pulled his head back under his shell a little, as if an old pain had been renewed. "Well, there came an autumn—October, it was—and on one afternoon both Ned and I realized that the whole west side had been built up just in one summer, while our backs were turned, you might say. That dreadful afternoon when we knew! For the first time I saw fear come in those beautiful great brown eyes of his. And my heart just shrank up inside me. I said to him, 'Ned, you'll have to go. No question about it. You wait till dark—and then run! There's probably only a couple of rows of houses—you can get past them to the reservoir.' Ned didn't say anything—just nodded. And we started to work our way toward where the brook comes in. I can't go back there any more—too much old sadness left for me there."

Simon Turtle cleared his throat, and went on. "That night came chill and misty—which was lucky, since Ned could hide in it. But he still couldn't bring himself to leave. We just stood there, beside the brook, and neither one of us said a word. At last I *had* to speak! I said, 'Go, Ned! For pity's sake—*run!*' He looked down on me, frowning that such a bad thing could happen—then, without a word, turned his back and ran. And I still hear his hoofs, at first on the turf and then on the streets the humans had built. It *is* something that you remember, you know—the sound of your best friend running away for dear life, when you know that you'll never see him again."

The turtle fell silent, reliving the awful experience. Then, having gotten through it once more, he drew a deep breath and said, "And that was so long ago— ages!—I can't even begin to remember the years. Poor Ned, poor Ned. The way they've been building since then, he's probably been pushed all the way up to Maine by now!"

"At least he escaped," said a small sad voice behind Tucker Mouse. "That's more than we can."

Tucker turned around. In back of him two funny little animals were sitting on their hind legs. They each had auburn fur and bright black eyes and worried expressions on their faces. "This is Henry Chipmunk and his sister Emily," said Chester.

"How do you do?" said Emily Chipmunk, and made a short bow to the new arrivals. She was a few years older than Henry and very polite.

"We're awfully glad you're here," said Henry. It was he who had spoken before. "We'll be safe now, won't we?"

"Well—I—I hope so." Tucker Mouse was a bit flustered by the confidence everyone had in him. He glanced around and saw that they were completely surrounded by the animals of the meadow. While the turtle had been telling his story of Ned Deer, the various rabbits and sundry fieldmice had gone all over, telling everyone they met that Chester's friends from the city had arrived and that now everything would be all right. "I certainly hope we can help you," said Tucker nervously.

"I *know* you can!" said someone above them. Halfway up the hill grew an elm tree. And one of its branches extended out over the pool. A squirrel was perched there.

"That's Bill," said Chester.

"Hi!" Bill Squirrel called down. As quick as blue fire, he ran back on the branch, down the trunk, and dashed over to join them. "Now what's the plan?"

"The plan?" Tucker looked helplessly at Harry Cat. "Harry—what's the plan?"

"You're the expert on the countryside," said Harry. "What *is* the plan?"

"Um—the plan." Tucker began thinking in earnest, pacing back and forth. "The plan, the plan—" And then suddenly he *did* have a plan! "Well, of course! The plan!" He shook his head at the ease of it all. "Really, Chester, it's so obvious I'm surprised you didn't think of it yourself."

"What?" "What?" "What?" shouted everyone at once.

"All Chester has to do is chirp!" announced the mouse. "I mean, chirp *human* music! When the people all realize that the famous cricket from Times Square is now living in Connecticut, and giving concerts again, they won't *dare* tear up his meadow!"

"Oh, Tucker, I *did* think of that already," said Chester.

"Oh, you did, did you?" said Tucker. He was secretly a little put out that someone had thought of his plan before him. "Then why didn't you do it?"

"It won't work," said the cricket. "In the first place, if I started giving concerts again, somebody would probably try to catch me. I wouldn't mind that, though. If living in a cage could save the meadow, I'd be glad to. But even if I wasn't caught—if I stayed right here— people would come pouring in to listen. You remember how crowded it got in the subway station when I played. Well, they'd come in cars, they'd come on foot, and they'd trample down everything! We want to keep the meadow the way it *is*."

"Hmm," mumbled Tucker Mouse. "I guess you're right."

"What's the next plan?" asked Bill Squirrel.

Tucker looked at all the faces that were staring at him hopefully. He shifted from one foot to the other. "I can't think of anything else. Right now."

Gloom spread among the animals. And whispers went back and forth: "No plan," "No other plan," "The mouse has no more plans."

The Old Meadow

Henry Chipmunk looked in Tucker's eyes a moment and then glanced away. "We were—we were sort of—counting on you, Mr. Mouse. Chester told us how smart you were, and we thought—we thought—" But his voice broke. He put his two little front paws up to his own eyes and began to cry.

"Now, now, Henry—don't do that." Chester Cricket patted the chipmunk on the back. He was so little that Henry could hardly feel it through his fur, but it helped, and the chipmunk stopped crying. "Tucker and Harry only got here today. They'll think of something before too long. Why don't all you folks go home now? And try not to worry—it'll just take a little time."

Gradually the animals dispersed. As the chipmunks were turning to go, Emily said to Tucker and Harry, "Won't you both please come and visit us some time? We live over in the west there—in the cellar of the old farm house."

"Delighted to," said Harry Cat. Tucker said nothing.

When everyone had left, Simon Turtle craned his head toward the mouse and said, "Don't be too upset now. That Henry's still a very young chipmunk. They're an emotional breed, too. Always were."

Tucker Mouse shook his head. "That was the worst thing that ever happened to me. Worse than being trampled on in the subway. I never saw a chipmunk cry before."

"You never saw a chipmunk before!" said Harry Cat.

45

"But it was the crying that got me, Harry," said Tucker. He stamped his foot impatiently. And it was only himself that he was impatient with. "We've *got* to think of something, Harry! We've just got to!"

"Now take it easy, Mousiekins." Harry Cat put his paw on Tucker's back—but gently this time. "We will."

FOUR

Ellen

The worried silence in which Harry, Tucker, Chester, and Simon Turtle were sitting was broken by a wild chattering in the elm tree above them. Bill Squirrel had returned to his branch, but now he began jumping around furiously as he shouted down at them, "Watch out! Here comes—"

Before he could finish, the others saw what was coming; a huge Saint Bernard dog bounded over the top of the hill, paused, saw Harry Cat, and charged down on him like a locomotive. It was just at this moment that Tucker learned whether he could swim or not—because Harry, in his sudden fright, knocked his friend over into the brook. It turned out that Tucker *could* swim. He paddled, spluttering, back to the bank just in time to see Harry Cat, who had no escape, take a good claw at the tender nose of the Saint Bernard. The big dog reared back on his hind legs, and Harry—a neat piece of strategy—dashed right between them, up the hill, and up the tree trunk to the safety of a high branch. The dog ran back after him, barking with rage. Two or three times he jumped up as far as he could on the trunk of the elm, but fell back helpless. Harry was well out of reach.

"Nice, peaceful meadow you've got here, Chester!" said Tucker Mouse, as he shook what water he could out of his fur.

"That was *awful!*" said the cricket. "Ellen and the little kids don't usually come over until the afternoon."

"Who's Ellen?" said Tucker.

"That's her." Chester pointed up to the top of the hill. A girl had appeared there. With her were four smaller children, two boys and two girls. "The little kids are Nancy, Anne, Jaspar, and John."

Up on the hill Ellen was scolding the Saint Bernard. "Stop that! Stop that barking, Ruff! Bad dog!—to chase the kitty like that."

"Bad dog! Bad dog!" One of the little boys joined in the scolding. He made a fist with his right hand, heaved back, and then socked the dog right in the jaw.

"Wow!" said Tucker Mouse. "That little guy better watch what he's doing!"

"It's all right," said Chester. "The dog belongs to his family. He's Jaspar. Ruff loves him."

Just as Chester had said, Ruff, the Saint Bernard, seemed to regard Jaspar's sock as no more than a love pat. He leaned over and gave the boy such a sloppy,

big kiss that it sent him rolling down the hill. Jaspar enjoyed his rolling, however, and helped it along, aiming himself right toward the bank of the pool.

"Don't you roll in that water, Jaspar!" shouted Ellen.

Jaspar stopped himself on the very brink. He stood up and said glumly, "I never get to do *nothin'!*"

" 'I never get to do *anything*,' " Ellen corrected him. "And you do so! You do everything you shouldn't." She looked up at Harry sitting on a branch of the tree. "Here, Kittykittykittykitty! Come down—I won't let the big dog hurt you."

Harry miaowed to her. She didn't understand, of course, but Tucker and Chester did. He was saying, "I think I'll stay right here for a while, thank you."

"Let's go down to the Special Place," Ellen said to the smaller children. "That'll give the kitty a chance to come down. Jaspar, you make sure Ruff stays with us."

"So *stay with us!*" Jaspar shouted at the dog. He lifted one ear and went *"Boo!"* inside it. But Ruff couldn't be made angry. He barked happily at the teasing. With Ellen and the others he went off down the other side of the hill, away from the pool.

Chester and Tucker climbed up the hill and reached the foot of the tree just as Harry was scrambling down. "Well, *that* was an invigorating experience!" said the cat.

Ellen

"What did the brute say while he was chasing you?" asked Tucker.

"He didn't say anything," said Harry Cat. "He just barked. I think he's lived around human beings so long he's forgotten how to talk to other animals."

"Serves him right!" muttered Tucker.

"You aren't hurt, are you, Harry?" said Chester. "He isn't a *bad* dog, really."

"No, I'm not hurt," said Harry Cat. "And I know he isn't a bad dog. He's just doing what dogs in Connecticut *do*—which is chase cats. I think it's awfully primitive, though. At least that girl liked me."

"She's always wanted a cat," said Chester. "Right over there is where she and her parents, Mr. and Mrs. Hadley, live." From the top of the hill the animals could see across the road that ran beside the meadow in the east. Opposite them, on the other side, stood a white house with green trim.

"Are they any relation to the man the town is named after?" asked Tucker.

"No. That was Joseph *Hedley*," said Chester. "Their name is *Hadley*. Ellen is the only one of the big kids that the mothers will let take the little kids over to the meadow. You see, in this neighborhood there are big kids and little kids. The little kids like the meadow, but when they get to be big kids, they usually would rather go off to the school yard and play baseball if they're boys, and if they're girls, they—they—"

"They what?" said Tucker.

"Well, they do whatever girls do!" said Chester. "But Ellen still loves it here, even though she's a big kid by now."

"How old is she?" said Harry.

"Oh—at least twelve."

"Mmm!" purred the cat. "Really getting on, isn't she?"

"And the mothers all trust her. So they let her bring the little kids over," said Chester. "They have a Special Place where they like to sit on the other side of the hill. Come on—I'll show you."

Silently—Harry was especially quiet, so that Ruff wouldn't notice him—the three of them crept over the hill. There was a glen on the other side, dotted with different kinds of trees. The brook flowed through, on its way to Simon's Pool, and just before it left the hollow, it made a bend around a plot of land where seven birch trees were growing in a circle. The earth was spongy and comfortable between them, covered with soft grass. This was Ellen's Special Place—her favorite spot in all the meadow. She and the four smaller children were sitting there now. Chester, Harry, and Tucker edged up through the shrubs to listen.

"I don't understand," one of the little girls was saying. "How can it be magic?"

"It just is," said Ellen. "There's magic all over the meadow. But especially right here."

Ellen

"Magic like what witches and wizards have?" asked John, the other little boy.

"No, not that kind," said Ellen.

"Then it ain't magic!" said Jaspar.

"'It isn't magic,'" said Ellen. "But it *is!* It's—it's something you *feel,* that's all."

Everyone was silent a moment and concentrated on feeling as much as he or she could. In one of the birches an oriole sang. Bright patches of sunlight danced around them, filtered through flickering branches and leaves. The brook rustled past them, whispering secrets continuously.

"I feel it," said the first little girl.

"So do I," said the second.

"Phooey!" Jaspar gave up on magic and began to wrestle with Ruff. The Saint Bernard let himself be pinned a few times—then he rolled Jaspar over on his stomach and pacified him with one big paw on his back, just the way Harry quieted Tucker Mouse.

"Anyway," said Jaspar from under the paw, "that magic better work! 'Cause if it doesn't, there isn't going to *be* any meadow! My dad says it'll all be built up in a year."

Ellen frowned and winced, as if she had been hit on a spot that was already sore. "No, it *won't* be built up!" she said. "That's just talk."

"What's going to stop them?" said Jaspar.

"I don't know. But something will," said Ellen.

"Hedley wouldn't be *Hedley* without the Old Meadow."

Over in the bushes Tucker whispered to Chester, "She's on our side!"

"I just wish there were more like her," Chester whispered back.

"Tucker, you've got to come up with something— for her sake, too!" said Harry Cat. He pushed aside a reed to get a better look.

Ellen heard the rustling and saw Harry's whiskered face peeking out. "Shh! No one move," she said to the children. "There's the kitty. Now I'm going to take you all home—"

"We just got here!" exclaimed Jaspar.

"I know," said Ellen. "But it's almost lunchtime anyway. And I'll bring you back this afternoon—I promise! I want to come back by myself and see if I can make friends with the kitty. He'll never come out with Ruff and all of you here. Come on now—please."

She led the children up the hill and over to the edge of the road. "Everyone take hands." The children fell into formation—two on each side of her—and all took hands. Ellen took a long look up and down the road. "Quick now—over!"

"You, too!" shouted Jaspar at Ruff.

And the six of them, Ruff included, hurried across the road. From there, since there were no more roads to cross, the children could find their way home by themselves. But Ellen came back and sat down again in her Special Place. Sometimes she liked being there alone even more than with the children.

"Here, kitty!" she called. "Come on. I won't hurt you."

"You made a big hit with her," said Tucker to Harry Cat.

"I'm going over and say hello," said Harry. "It'll make her happy."

"It'll make *you* happy!" said Tucker Mouse disgustedly. "You're just looking for a little free admiration. Mister Kitty!"

Harry padded out over the grass and sat down beside Ellen. "Well, *hello!*" she said, and began stroking Harry's head. "You're a *nice* kitty, aren't you? Yes! You're a *beautiful* kitty!"

Tucker Mouse grimaced at Chester. "I wonder what she'd say if she knew that that 'beautiful kitty' lived in a drain pipe in the subway station!"

"I don't think it makes any difference where you live," said Chester. "If you're nice, you're nice. And Harry *is* a nice kitty."

"Cat! He's a cat!" shouted Tucker Mouse, who was actually a little jealous of all the attention his friend was getting. "Don't use that obnoxious baby talk!" Chester tried not to laugh, and Tucker went on ranting. "Just look at the way he's buttering up to her, arching his head up under her hand like that! And miaowing like a movie star! I never thought I'd see the day!"

Ellen had taken Harry into her lap and was stroking his back from his head all the way down to his tail. And, in fact, Harry Cat *was* enjoying the whole thing very much. With each new stroke he let out a loud purr of pleasure.

"You have no collar, do you, kitty?" said Ellen. Harry purred. "And I've never seen you in this neighborhood before. Are you lost?" Harry purred. "Would you like to come home with me? I'd fix you up a bed of blankets in my room. And I'd give you all delicious things to eat. Would you like to be my kitty?" Harry purred and rolled over to have his stomach rubbed.

"Come on then!" said Ellen. She picked Harry up and began to walk up the hill.

"Hey! What's she doing?" shouted Tucker Mouse. "Chester—look! Do something! Stop her! Quick!"

"What can I do?" said Chester.

"But she's kidnapping Harry Cat!" said Tucker.

"He doesn't look too unhappy about it," said the cricket.

And that certainly was true. For Harry Cat was lying over one of Ellen's arms, as limp and content as laundry on the line.

FIVE

Harry the House Cat

Tucker spent the rest of his first full day in Connecticut fuming about Harry Cat and blowing his nose on fern handkerchiefs. When Ellen came back to the meadow that afternoon with the little kids, she did not bring Harry with her. But she told them all about how she had made friends with the kitty that morning, and how nice he was, and how she had brought him home and her mother had said she could keep him a few days on trial, and then, if things worked out all right, she could keep him permanently.

Tucker was hiding over in the bushes with Chester, listening. "I can't understand it," he said. "Why doesn't Harry fight to get out? Why doesn't he bite, scratch, claw—?"

"And he just loves to have his tummy rubbed!" said Ellen to the children.

"That's the answer," said Chester.

Tucker growled something unpleasant—as much as

a mouse can growl, that is—and said he was sure Harry would escape before the day was done.

But evening came on, and Harry did not return. And night followed, and still the cat did not come back. Chester and Tucker went back to the stump. Instead of the human food that he scrounged from the lunch stands in the subway station, which was what he really liked, Tucker had to content himself with some nuts and seeds that Chester had collected for him in the meadow. And later, when he tried to sleep, the noise of the brook, which had sounded like laughter in the daylight, kept him awake most of the night.

"Subways I can sleep through," he grumbled to himself. "Commuters I can sleep through. But that brook just goes on—and on—and on!"

The countryside did not seem nearly so charming as it had in the morning.

Next day the sun rose bright and strong. And it woke Tucker up as soon as it climbed above the horizon. One crafty ray darted in through the hole in the stump and landed right in the mouse's eye. Like most city people, Tucker Mouse was not in the habit of getting up with the sun.

"Neon lights I can sleep through," he groaned as he heaved himself awake, "but not that sun!"

Chester Cricket, who *was* in the habit of getting up at dawn, had already been down to have his wash in the brook. Tucker Mouse staggered down to the edge of the stream, took a drink, and blew his nose, which still was running, on a convenient fern. "Did Harry come back?" he asked.

"I don't see any sign of him," said Chester.

"Well, this has got to stop!" exclaimed the mouse. "We have to go over to the Hadleys' house and see what's happening! They may have him tied up."

"All right, all right, Tucker," said Chester. "Just keep calm. I'm sure he's safe."

"I *am* calm!" shouted the mouse, and marched off toward Tuffet Country.

Chester had a hard time keeping up with him. By the time they had gone through Pasture Land, past Simon's Pool, up the hill, and across the road to reach the Hadleys' lawn, the cricket was panting. "Whoa, Tucker!" He gave a last big hop and sat still. "We've got to think what we're going to do."

"Bust the front door down if necessary!" said the mouse.

"Why don't we go around to the sun porch instead," said Chester. "Maybe we can get Harry's attention without anyone seeing."

"Okay," said Tucker. "But I'm warning you—I'm not leaving here without Harry!"

They crept around to the rear of the house. On one side there was a sun porch, and only a screen door separated it from the warm summer outside. Chester and Tucker peered in. And there, sprawled out on a cushion obviously laid down for him, was Harry Cat, snoozing in a pool of sunlight. "Harry!" whispered Tucker urgently. "Harry, wake up! It's us!"

Harry Cat opened one eye, saw who it was, and came padding over to his side of the screen door. "Well, well!" he purred. "It's my friends from the country. How's life in the wide-open spaces?"

Tucker ignored the teasing tone in his friend's voice and said angrily, "What are you doing in there?"

"Waiting for breakfast," said Harry Cat. He gave Chester a quick look and a grin. "Supper was so delicious last night—I can't wait to see what we're having this morning!"

"Supper?" A sad and soulful look came over the face of Tucker Mouse. "What did you have for supper?"

"Well, they didn't have any cat food in the house, so they gave me what they had themselves."

"And what was that, may I ask?" said Tucker.

"A little bit of shrimp cocktail first—"

"Harry, stop it. I changed my mind—I don't want to hear."

"—and then roast beef and French-fried potatoes and cauliflower with a marvelous cream and cheese sauce—"

"Harry, please! You wouldn't do this to me, please."

"—and for dessert—they all thought it was delight-

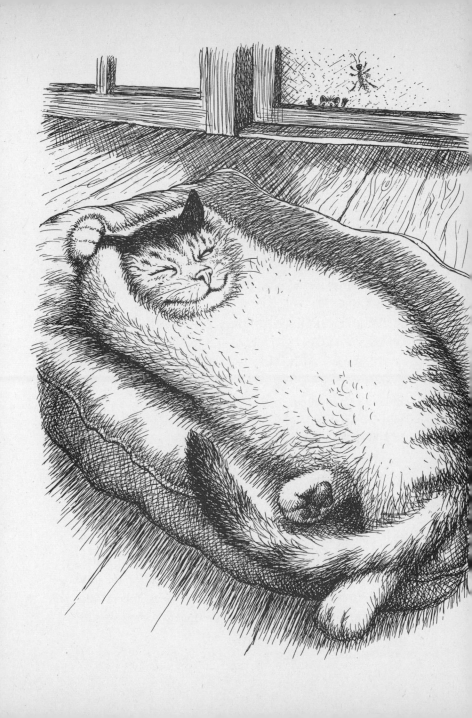

ful to see a kitty eating dessert—they gave me vanilla ice cream—"

"*Harry!*"

"—with chocolate sauce." Harry finished his narration of delicacies and smiled out at Tucker. "Wasn't that nice of them?"

Tucker turned to Chester Cricket. "Who would have thought an old friend could be so cruel?" Chester, who was trying not to laugh, just shrugged.

"What did you two have for supper?" asked Harry.

Tucker made a wry face. "A few wild nuts and seeds."

"Wild nuts and seeds!" purred Harry. "That sounds pleasantly rustic."

"Pleasantly rustic they may have been—you would excuse me, please, Chester—but not very filling to a mouse accustomed to scrounging around some of the best lunch stands in New York!"

Harry suddenly looked into the living room, which an open door connected with the sun porch. "Shh!" he warned. "Here comes Ellen. Hide in that hedge beside the screen door."

Tucker and Chester disappeared into a privet hedge just as Ellen stepped out into the sun porch. She was carrying a saucer piled with smoking bacon and eggs. "Mother said she'd get some regular cat food at the store today," she said to Harry as she set the saucer in front of him. "But in the meantime would you like some bacon and eggs?"

Harry the House Cat

"Mmm!" purred Harry Cat.

Ellen went to the screen door and looked out. An east wind had begun to lift clouds, a gray mountain range of them, up into the sky. "If it's nice, we'll go over to the meadow this morning," she said to Harry. "And if it rains, I'll brush you again." She went back into the main part of the house, to have her own breakfast.

Before it was even safe, Tucker Mouse darted out of the privet hedge and had his nose pressed against the screen door. "See what I mean about the food?" said Harry. Very casually he began to chew a piece of bacon. "Nice and crisp—just the way I like it."

Tucker's mouth began to water. "Harry Cat, are you going to sit there and eat that right in front of me?" he asked indignantly.

"You want me to turn my back?" said Harry.

"No!" shouted the mouse. "I want you to give me some!"

"Well, perhaps I *could* open the door," said Harry, but he didn't sound too convinced.

"You'd better," said Chester. "Or else he'll gnaw a hole right through the screen to get at that food!"

Harry laughed and stood up on his hind legs. The latch of a screen door presented no problems at all to such a big, clever cat, and in a moment he had opened it wide enough for Tucker to scramble in over the sill. The mouse ran toward the bacon and eggs and almost dove in.

"Tasty, eh?" said Harry.

"De-*glicious!*" mumbled Tucker through a mouthful.

Harry offered Chester some breakfast, but the cricket refused. He didn't mind a bite of human food now and then in New York, but in Connecticut he preferred the things that grew in the meadow.

After the cat and the mouse had finished eating— Tucker did most of the eating, Harry only got half a piece of bacon—the mouse licked off his whiskers and said, "Okay, that was good. But let's get going."

"Yes, you'd better be going," said Harry Cat.

Tucker stared at him. "What do you mean, '*You'd* better be going.' Aren't you coming too?"

"Well, if it doesn't rain, I may see you in the meadow," said Harry. He glanced out the screen door. "I think it's going to, though. In that case, Ellen will probably spend the morning brushing me. How do you like my coat, by the way? Beautiful, hmm? She brushed me for two hours last night. With her mother's best hairbrush at that."

"You mean you're going to *stay?*" exclaimed Tucker.

"Of course I'm going to stay," said Harry. "I like it here. After the brushing we'll have tummy-rubbing time."

"I can't believe it!" Tucker looked out the screen door at Chester in amazement, then back at Harry Cat, who was sitting primly on his hind legs, the very

picture of a domestic pet. "Abandoning his friends—
for the sake of a few material comforts!"

"Which you ate most of," said Harry.

Tucker shook his head. "But, Harry—a big, husky
tomcat like you, the terror of Forty-second Street—"

"—and now I'm just a Connecticut house cat."
Harry sighed. "Well, that's the way it happens sometimes." He swished his tail neatly around his front
legs. "If you'll excuse me now, I think I'll go have
a bowl of heavy cream."

That was too much for Tucker. *"Harry Cat, you stay
right where you are!"* he shouted.

"Now take it easy, Mousiekins," said Harry in a
voice that sounded more like his own and less like a
Connecticut house cat. "Look at the advantages if I
stay with the Hadleys. I can swipe you some Kleenexes
to blow your nose on instead of those ferns. And I can
also smuggle you out some human food. I believe Mrs.
Hadley said they were having hamburgers for lunch."

"Hamburgers—" That same dreamy expression
appeared on Tucker's face again.

"And I can also be a spy," said Harry, speaking more
to Chester now. "Last night Mr. Hadley was reading
the newspaper, and he said that someone in the Town
Council had proposed that they build apartment
houses in the Old Meadow."

"Apartment houses!" said Chester. "That's the worst
yet!"

"This article he was reading said that lots of people were moving into town—some factory or other opened up somewhere—and the Old Meadow was the only undeveloped area left. Now if I was living here, I could follow developments and report them to you. How about it, Chester?" Harry looked at Tucker. "How about it, Tucker?"

"What are they having for supper tonight?" said Tucker Mouse.

"Probably lobster Newburg!" said Harry. "Think of me as a spy and a food thief, not a house cat—it'll make it easier for you. But you have to make up your mind right now—here comes Ellen again!"

"All right, all right—stay!" said Tucker, and scuttled through the crack left open in the screen door. He poked his head back in just long enough to say, "And don't forget the sauce!"

Ellen came into the sun porch. "It *is* going to rain, kitty. It's started already. We'll have to spend the day indoors. But I don't mind. There're lots of games we can play." She lifted Harry up and carried him to the screen door. Drops were beginning to sparkle on the grass and the privet hedge. "Aren't you glad that you're not out there in the wet?" said Ellen.

"Mmm!" purred Harry Cat. He looked out in the back yard, where he knew Tucker and Chester were watching him, and winked.

66

SIX

Flood

The rain began as a soft, gray, summer shower. Tucker and Chester trudged home through it, and by the time they reached the tree stump, they both were soaked. Life was quiet in the meadow when it rained. The various rabbits and sundry fieldmice stayed in their holes. And gone was the usual glitter and bustle of insects, dragonflies, and water bugs beside the brook.

"I hope you won't get bored," said Chester. "There isn't much to do in the meadow when it rains."

"I'm not bored," said Tucker. He was looking out the hole in the stump, drying off. The rain, pushed by the wind's hand, swayed forward and back, like a curtain of silver. It fell on the roof of the stump and made a pattering sound. It fell on the grass, which seemed to turn even greener beneath it. And best of all, to Tucker's thinking, it fell in the brook. It struck him as somehow right and nice and complete that the water from the sky met the water on the earth. "Usually the only falling water I see is the dirty stuff that leaks out of the drain pipes in the walls of the subway station," said Tucker. "But this is different. I like to watch this rain."

And that is what he did all day long.

And the next morning, when they both woke up, it still was raining. It tapered off a little toward noon, however, and Tucker insisted that they go over to the Hadleys' and see if there were any further plans for building in the meadow. (Also, although he didn't mention it, he was rather interested in what had been eaten in the Hadley home just lately.)

The trip over was not so easy as it had been yesterday. Chester hopped from the top of one tuffet to another, while Tucker had to slosh through puddle after puddle. Pasture Land, too, was soggy and treacherous. But the going became easier when they reached the hill above Simon's Pool, and at last they arrived in the Hadleys' back yard.

There was no one home. Tucker looked in at the screen door and whispered, "Psst! Harry, it's us." When there was no answer, he said louder, "Harry, where are you?" And finally he ended up shouting, *"Harry Cat, you come out here!"*

"They're all gone," said Chester, who had hopped down to the end of a flagstone path that led to the garage. "The car's not there. They must be at the market. Harry, too."

"Market," said Tucker sadly, thinking of all the rows

68

and rows of good things to eat. "I wish I was at the market."

They waited under the privet hedge for almost an hour. But the Hadleys did not come back, and it began to rain harder. The open earth where they were sitting turned into streaming mud.

"We'd better go home," said Chester. "We're going to get drenched as it is."

"Drenched!" exclaimed Tucker Mouse. He was sopping wet, his whiskers were drooping, and he looked altogether bedraggled. "I couldn't get any more drenched if I went swimming again! Which I'm not, thank you!" But he, too, agreed that they ought to return to the stump.

Getting back was even harder than coming to the Hadleys' house had been. In just the short time they'd been gone, Tuffet Country had turned into a shallow lake, the tuffets sticking up like islands. Tucker had said that he would not go swimming, but that, in fact, was what he did. Where the water wasn't too deep, he could wade. But when it got over his head, he had to paddle as best he could. Chester waited for him on the tops of the tuffets where he landed.

"This is awful!" said the cricket.

"I'll say!" said Tucker. He came puffing up to a bit of land that was still out of water below one tuffet, and collapsed for a rest.

"First Harry gets chased by a Saint Bernard—and now you have to practically *swim* home!"

Flood

"Oh, well," said Tucker bravely, "I didn't expect life in the wild to be easy." He took a deep breath and felt as much like a pioneer as he could. "Shall we push on?"

They pushed on and finally reached the stump. Fortunately the rain was slanting away from the hole, so the insides were still dry and comfortable. Tucker lay on a pile of wood chips, getting his breath back. "I'm turning into a champion athlete," he said. He gave a cough and patted himself on the chest. "My wind's still not what it should be, though." As he rested, he became aware of a rushing sound outside. "What's that noise?" he asked.

Chester hopped to the hole. "It's just the brook. It speeds up when there's more water in it."

Tucker crawled over and looked out, too. It was still the same brook—but somehow different. "It doesn't look the way it should," said the mouse.

Chester was silent a minute, studying the stream. Then he said, "I think the water level's rising."

"Hmm," said Tucker. He looked at Chester, then down at the hurrying current beneath them. "I keep saying these things as jokes—but maybe I *am* going to become a champion swimmer!"

It was no joke. Five days later Tucker Mouse wished that he *was* a champion swimmer. Or, better still, he wished that he and Chester hadn't come back from the Hadleys' house when they went to look for Harry

Cat. Or, best of all, he wished that he and the cat hadn't come to Connecticut in the first place!

No one in the meadow could remember anything like it: it rained almost steadily for six days! Now lighter, now heavier, now seeming as if it was about to stop, but never stopping, the rain just kept coming. Sometimes the clouds opened up a little, a bit of blue was seen, a few stray sunbeams struck the stump—but then the clouds would close again, and water, always more water, fell.

If Tuffet Country had been a lake on the second day, when Chester and Tucker woke up on the third day, they looked out over a positive ocean. Only the tallest tuffets stood up above the surface. And beyond them the mouse and the cricket could see that Pasture Land was flooded, too. They decided not even to try to get to the Hadleys' house that day. But if they'd known what was in store for them, they would have swum and floundered up to the high ground above Simon's Pool any way they could.

The brook had risen steadily for the first four days. Then it had leveled off. Its channel was broad and deep and could accommodate the torrent that now raced through it. But Chester kept a sharp eye on the water level nonetheless. There was something that worried him—but he didn't mention it to Tucker Mouse.

Now, on the afternoon of the sixth day of rain, the

Flood

two of them sat looking out of the hole at the waste
of water all around. "Trapped!" said Tucker Mouse.
"Like rats in traps we're trapped!" He sighed. "I'll
never insult my nice leaking drain pipes again."

"It *can't* last much longer," said Chester.

"That's what you said three days ago—four days
ago—*five* days ago! And *look* at it!" exclaimed the
mouse. Chester said nothing. What could he say? It
was true. "Are there any more nuts or seeds?" asked
Tucker.

"We ate the last yesterday," said Chester. "But
don't worry—we won't go hungry. John Robin said
he'd bring us something if we ran out."

"Tell him to make mine a bacon, lettuce, and
tomato sandwich," said Tucker grimly.

The one bright spot in the whole soggy experience
had been John Robin. He had his nest in the willow
tree next to Chester's stump, and he dropped in every
day to give them the news. It was from him that they
learned that the various rabbits and sundry fieldmice
had moved up to the hill above the pool. A lot of
burrows had been washed away, but so far no one had
been killed. And over on the other side of the brook,
where the land was a little higher, the folks were pretty
damp, he said, but they weren't suffering too much.

"I can't stand it any more!" said Tucker after
another hour of watching the flood. "I'm going to jump
for it and swim."

"Don't!" said Chester. "The current's much too strong in the brook—and you'd never make it all the way across the parts that are sunk."

"But I can't *stand it!*" groaned Tucker. He was about to launch into a lengthy description of what he couldn't stand—the boredom, the hunger—when suddenly the whole stump trembled as if it had been struck. "Hey, what's that?" said the mouse. He looked down and saw that just in the last few minutes the brook had abruptly risen much higher. Waves, some of them uncomfortably large, were beginning to pound at the base of the stump. "What's going on?"

Chester Cricket shook his head. "Now don't get nervous, Tucker, but I think that maybe—"

"Chester! Tucker!" John Robin appeared from nowhere and perched on the edge of the hole. "The reservoir's overflowing!"

Tucker looked at Chester. "Is that what you were thinking maybe?"

"It's what I've been afraid of all week," said the cricket.

"So now what happens?"

"Well, it depends on how much it's overflowing."

"Pouring over the spillway like crazy!" said John Robin helpfully.

"Uh—Tucker—I think perhaps we ought to get up on top of the stump," said Chester.

74

Flood

"You mean you think it could come all the way up to the *hole?*" said Tucker.

"Never saw such a waterfall in my life!" said the robin.

"Please, John, you needn't give us the details," said Tucker. "Just get out of the way so we can climb on the roof!" John fluttered up on to the stump, and Tucker and Chester clambered after him. From out there the view of the wide lake the Old Meadow had become was even less to Tucker's liking. "Now what?" he said.

"Now we wait," said Chester.

And wait they did—as the torrent below them frothed higher and higher around the stump. John Robin kept flying off to the reservoir—no trip at all as a robin flies—and coming back with encouraging news like "Even more water coming over now!" and "Looks as if the whole thing may give way!" The only hopeful thing to occur was that late in the afternoon the thick curtain of clouds did finally lift. A broad band of blue sky appeared in the west, grew larger, and in a few minutes the sunlight, dense and warm, was glittering over the acres of water.

"I think it's actually cleared up!" said Chester.

"Beautiful!" said Tucker. "We'll have a nice, sunny day to get drowned in." By now the water was beginning to lap over the top of the stump. "Listen, Chester

—there's no point in having both of us go down with the stump. You're little—John Robin can carry you up to his nest. Didn't you say you had a nest up there, John?"

The robin pointed to one of the branches of the willow tree that overhung Chester's stump. "That's me—third branch from the top on the left."

"Now Tucker," Chester began, "I will *not* leave—"

"A moment, please," said Tucker. He was feeling very noble and tragic and wanted to deliver a little eulogy on himself. "Never let it be said that Tucker Mouse allowed a friend of his to be sacrificed needlessly. And speaking of friends—" His tone changed considerably. "—if you can catch Harry Cat some time when he isn't being brushed or having his tummy rubbed, you can tell him what a bum I think he is! Tell him if he ever decides to go back to New York, I leave all my Life Savings to him–he can buy his very own tummy-rubber with them!—and tell him I hope he enjoyed the lobster Newburg!"

Chester ignored Tucker's outburst. The sight of the willow tree had given him an idea. "John, some of those branches are hanging right over us. And willow branches are nice and bendy, too. If you flew up to that lowest one there, maybe your weight would push it down far enough so Tucker and I could grab it."

"I'll try." The robin flew up and got a grip on the branch. It lowered a bit but still remained high above the stump. "I'm not heavy enough!" the robin called down.

"Go get lots of birds!" shouted the cricket. "And hurry! The water's already over our feet."

"And tell him I went down proudly! A proud mouse to the end!" said Tucker, who still was ranting at Harry Cat. "A valiant fight I fought—while *he* was lounging around on cushions!"

Chester began to lose his patience. "Oh, Tucker, stop raving! We're not going to drown!"

"We're not?" Tucker seemed surprised and a little miffed that his heroism might not be necessary.

"Just get ready to grab that branch."

When the water had risen to Chester's knees—but a cricket's knees are not very high—John Robin flew back. With him were two sparrows, the oriole who lived in the trees above Ellen's Special Place, and a grackle named Sam. They all clung to the branch. It drooped down farther but was still above the heads of Chester and Tucker.

"Not low enough," called Chester. "Ask Beatrice to come over." The robin flew off.

"Who's Beatrice?" said Tucker.

"A pheasant who lives in the woods on the other side of the brook," said Chester. "She's the biggest bird in the meadow."

The water was up to Chester's shoulders when John flew back with Beatrice Pheasant. When she settled on the branch, it sank down within reach of Tucker's front claws, if he stood on his hind legs. He boosted Chester up, the cricket got a grip, and then Tucker too grabbed hold with both claws for dear life. "Now all you birds fly off one by one, or we'll be flipped all the way back to New York!" said Tucker. He sighed to himself. "We should be so lucky!"

One by one the birds left the branch. And very slowly, steadily, the mouse and the cricket were lifted up, as if by a firm, sure hand, till they hung amid the branches of the willow tree. Beatrice Pheasant was the last one off. When her weight was gone, Chester and Tucker were able to transfer from their elevator branch to a larger one nearby—the one on which John Robin had his nest.

"Wheeoo!" groaned Tucker with relief. "Thanks for the help, Miss Pheasant."

"*Mrs.* Pheasant!" said Beatrice proudly. She had a good heart, but she was very conscious of the position she and her husband occupied as the two least common birds in the meadow. "Jerome is back in the woods, minding the children."

"Well, tell your husband I'm glad he's got such a—" Tucker was about to say "fat wife"—for Beatrice Pheasant was indeed a very large bird—but he stopped himself in time. "Plump helpmeet" was the only other thing he could think of, but that didn't sound right either.

"Just tell him thank you for letting you come over," said Chester.

"We'd do anything for you, Chester," said the pheasant. "Or for any friend of yours. Although, Mr. Mouse," she went on reproachfully, "you don't seem to be having much luck in saving the meadow, do you?"

"Please, Mrs. Pheasant, you wouldn't rub it in. I'm doing the best I can. Right now I'd just like to stay alive for a while!"

Beatrice Pheasant spread her beautiful auburn wings, held them poised a moment—probably so Tucker could admire them—and then flew off over the brook toward the woods.

"Climb on back to the nest," said John Robin. "You can stay with us till the flood goes down."

Very carefully Tucker inched his way along the branch, mumbling to himself. "I go swimming—I climb trees—*oh!*" He caught a glimpse of the water swirling far beneath him, and hung on tighter. "And me with my fear of heights! This is no life for a mouse from New York."

Near the willow's trunk John Robin had his nest. It was occupied by John's wife Dorothy and three young robins, who were very surprised to see a mouse come climbing into their home. "Move over," said the mouse. "Your Uncle Tucker has come for a visit!"

Chester hopped in after him. "Now the first thing to

do is for John to fly over and tell Harry that we're all right."

"Let him wait," said Tucker. "Let him worry awhile." But Chester nodded to John, and the robin flickered off in the direction of the Hadleys' house. Tucker went on sulking, though. "He's probably over in that sun porch having a chocolate sundae right now!"

SEVEN

Indoors

And so, after having spent almost all his first week in Connecticut in Chester's stump, trapped by the flood, Tucker Mouse spent almost all his second week in a robin's nest, waiting for the waters to subside. It wasn't altogether unpleasant, however. The three young robins proved to be a very enthusiastic audience. Tucker told them stories of his life in New York— how he sometimes rode the shuttle from Times Square to Grand Central Station, just for the fun of it, and how exciting it was to scrounge for the small change that the human beings lost, especially during rush hour. The three youngsters were so thrilled that one morning they announced to their mother, Dorothy Robin, that when they grew up they were going to New York and live in the Times Square subway station. Dorothy was a sensible robin, and a very good mother too, so she didn't tell them that they could *not* go to New York. She just kept feeding them the worms that she plucked up from the lawns of the houses across the street, and told them she thought it would be best if they waited until they were grown up before they decided where they wanted to live.

Chester and Tucker didn't have to eat worms to survive. John Robin brought them nuts and seeds, and by the time their stay in the willow was over, Tucker had actually gotten to like them—although he still missed the human food he was used to. For diversion he also learned to climb around on the branches of the willow tree. "Who would have thought it?" he said to himself. "An underground mouse like me—and now I'm a champion tree climber and swimmer!"

The flood gradually receded, and a day came at last when dry land appeared in the meadow. Chester and Tucker thanked the robins for their hospitality, promised to come back for a visit very soon, and scrambled down, branch by branch, to the earth beneath the willow tree.

"Doesn't it feel wonderful to be on solid ground again?" said Chester.

"I'll say!" Tucker answered. The first thing they did was to examine Chester's stump, which still was dampish, but drying out nicely, and the second was— "Harry Cat!" said Tucker. "Let's go!"

They found him waiting for them at the sun-porch door. "I knew you'd be coming over," said Harry. "I've been watching the flood from Mrs. Hadley's bedroom window, and I saw you could make it today."

"Hmm!" sniffed Tucker. "From a safe bedroom window he watches the scene of our peril! Is there anything to eat?"

"Yes," said Harry. "I saved something for you." He unlatched the door. "Come on in. It's safe—Mrs. Hadley and Ellen have gone over to Jaspar's house for lunch."

Chester and Tucker crept in, and Harry ushered the mouse over to a saucer placed in one corner of the sun porch. "Cat food!" exclaimed Tucker when he saw what was in the dish. "That's not what I want!"

"I'm sorry, Tucker," said Harry. "I wish it was sirloin steak—but they put me on cat food the day after I saw you last. Try it. It's tuna fish. You'll like it."

Tucker took a suspicious sniff at the tuna, then a less suspicious bite, and in a minute he was munching happily. "Not bad," he said. "Tastes sort of like the tuna-fish salad sandwiches they make at the lunch counters back home." He took an appraising glance at Harry and then said to Chester, "The kitty here has put on weight."

"You would have too, if you'd been eating the way I have," said Harry.

Tucker drew himself up proudly. "I, on the other hand, have *lost* weight. Did you notice what good shape I'm in, Harry? That comes from leading the outdoor life. See this muscle here? I got that from swimming. And this one here I got from climbing trees."

Indoors

"And that muscle in your jaw you got from talking too much," said Harry. "Why don't you use it to eat for a while?"

Tucker took one more look at his friend and shook his head sadly. "Pity to see a vigorous alley cat go flabby." Then he resumed his gobbling.

"I'm glad the Hadleys are treating you so well, Harry," said Chester.

"Oh, they treat me beautifully!" said the cat. "They're crazy about me—even Mr. Hadley. The only trouble is, they don't know my name is Harry, and they can't decide what to call me."

"I could think of a couple of names," said Tucker through a mouthful of tuna fish.

"Have you heard anything more about the meadow?" asked the cricket.

"No new plans yet," said Harry. "But Ellen told her mother that the flood did a lot of damage down where the brook flows out of the meadow—where we met you the first night. It almost washed away the bridge that the road goes over."

Chester shook his head. "That's bad. The human beings hate it worst of all when something interferes with their cars. I wish they liked meadows as much as they do roads."

"What's for dessert?" said Tucker, licking the last of the tuna fish off his whiskers.

"Nice to see that *you* still know what's important!" said Harry.

"I know it's important to save the meadow," said Tucker. "But to someone who has just spent two weeks in a stump and in a willow tree, surrounded by raging flood waters, dessert is also important!"

Harry sighed helplessly. "Come on," he said, and led the mouse and the cricket out of the sun porch, through the living room, and into the Hadleys' kitchen. The only sweet thing he could find, in one bottom cupboard, was a jar of preserves with its top screwed on loosely. So for dessert Tucker had two mouthfuls of strawberry jam.

When Tucker was full, and feeling much better, he took a long look around the kitchen. "You know, this is the first time I've ever been in a human being's house," he said. "I could do some very lovely scrounging here. Could we have a tour, Harry?"

Harry said he guessed it would be all right and took them both on an excursion through the Hadleys' home. First they crept down the cellar stairs, Chester Cricket hopping along behind the other two. And Tucker liked the basement very much. There were boxes piled everywhere, most of them empty, wood was stacked against the wall, Mrs. Hadley's freezer was purring in one corner, and in another there was a battered, old suitcase lying open. In it was a collection of the toys that Ellen had had when she was a little kid. Tucker pulled out a clawful of stuffing from a ripped Teddy bear, examined it closely, and pronounced, "Excellent for nesting!"

Indoors

After the cellar, the first and second floor were a disappointment. "Too neat," said Tucker. When Harry offered him a Kleenex from a box in Mrs. Hadley's bedroom, he declined, and told the cat that he didn't need to blow his nose any more. His hay fever had completely vanished when he became an athlete.

The climax of the trip was the attic. Tucker's eyes sparkled at what he saw: a welter of everything—books, bottles, old boxes—all lying around haphazard and helter-skelter. "Wow!" he exclaimed with admiration. "And I thought *my* house was a mess!" He began to pick his way lovingly through the debris. "This place is a rodent's paradise! I could spend the rest of my life here! What's this?" He stopped before a piece of wood that had iron letters nailed to it. They spelled H-A-D-L-E-Y.

Chester Cricket jumped over. "That's a sign the Hadleys used to have in their front yard, before the post it was on got broken. Lots of families in Connecticut have them—so people will know who lives where."

"Maybe I could have one outside the drain pipe in the subway station," said Tucker. "In beautiful gold letters: M-O-U-S-E!" He continued browsing happily among all the things that the Hadleys didn't need any more but couldn't bear to throw away: the treasure of attics everywhere.

Chester and Harry did some exploring too. Harry came across two old-fashioned pewter pots that he thought were very pretty and deserved a better fate than to be discarded and forgotten, and Chester found a box full of baby clothes. He guessed that they had once been worn by Ellen, or perhaps even her mother —they were so old that the colors had begun to fade and change.

It was a very happy time for the three of them. In fact, it was so happy that they forgot how long they'd been there.

Suddenly Harry Cat lifted his head. He'd been rummaging through Mr. Hadley's sports equipment—a tennis racket with loose strings, a broken golf club, things like that—and was about to suggest that Tucker Mouse, the great athlete, might find a use for some of them, but now he whispered urgently, "Shh!" A murmur of voices came from the floor below. "It's Ellen and her mother," said Harry. "They're back from lunch." He listened again. "They're in Mrs. Hadley's bedroom. Come on—I'll sneak you through the hall and downstairs."

Very quietly the animals tiptoed down the attic stairs. Harry peeked out: the hall was clear. They were just about to begin creeping down beside the banister of the staircase to the first floor when Mrs. Hadley said, "Oh dear—there it is!"

"There's what?" said Ellen.

The afternoon newspaper had been delivered while Ellen and her mother were out to lunch, and Mrs. Hadley was glancing over the front page. "It says here that the Town Council *has* decided to build apartment houses on the site of the Old Meadow."

"Oh, *no!*" said Ellen. She didn't know it, but out in the hall a cricket echoed her forlorn groan.

"It says that the recent flooding has proved that the area is 'a hazard to the community.'"

"Isn't there any other way they could stop the flooding?" said Ellen.

"I don't know, dear," her mother answered. She went on reading. " 'Plans are being made to level the entire meadow and construct a conduit for the brook passing through it. Work is expected to begin later on this summer.' " The animals were shocked by the news. They stood motionless at the top of the staircase. "Now try not to be too upset, dear," said Mrs. Hadley, her voice coming nearer the bedroom door. "I know how you feel, but—*a mouse!*"

Harry and Tucker plunged downstairs. Chester hopped after them, four steps at a time. But Mrs. Hadley wasn't concerned with the cat or the cricket— in fact, she didn't even notice Chester. Although her attic was a mess, and her cellar none too tidy either, she prided herself on keeping a clean house, and for her, mice spelled trouble. She ran to the hall closet, took out a broom, and chased Tucker, whacking at him as she went. Halfway downstairs she caught him and gave him such a whop that he tumbled, head over heels, the rest of the way. But he landed right side up and kept on running—through the living room, through the sun porch, and out the unlatched screen door. Mrs. Hadley charged after him and just caught a glimpse of his tail as Tucker vanished into the privet hedge.

"The very idea!" said Mrs. Hadley. "A mouse! Sitting right out plain in the hall! Just as bold as you please." At that very moment, although she didn't see it, a tiny black shape, Chester Cricket, jumped over Mrs. Hadley's foot and into the hedge.

Ellen came out into the yard carrying Harry. He looked around, saw that Tucker had escaped, and heaved a sigh of relief.

"And Ellen," Mrs. Hadley went on, "there's something very peculiar about that cat of yours. He was standing right next to the mouse, not doing a thing! Just as if they were the best friends in the world!"

"He may be peculiar, but he's nice!" said Ellen, and kissed Harry on the head.

In the Hadleys' front yard the mouse, next to whom that peculiar cat had been standing, was limping toward the road. He stopped to massage one hind leg. "That lady sure packs a wallop!" he said to the cricket hopping along beside him. "Wow! One Connecticut housewife—and she's worse than a whole herd of commuters! At evening rush hour, too!"

EIGHT

Bertha

News of its coming fate—apartment houses—spread quickly through the meadow. All the animals agreed that next to gas stations it was the worst thing that could happen. Individual houses would have been bad enough, but at least some of the smaller folk could have found homes in the shrubs and hedges around them. But with apartment houses—great, tall structures of brick and concrete—there wasn't much hope for anyone.

Secretly, although no one said so out loud, everyone was still hoping that Tucker Mouse could come up with a plan to save them. And Tucker knew it. When he went out walking and met Henry Chipmunk, he could tell from the hopeful way Henry said "Hello, Mr. Mouse!" that the chipmunk still had confidence in him. Henry was always asking him to come and visit him and his sister Emily in their home on the other side of the brook. But Tucker didn't go. It was too painful to be in the company of friends who trusted you to help them, when you didn't know how you could. Poor Tucker! He took long walks, and racked his brains—and became almost as fond of the Old Meadow as the animals who had lived their whole lives there—but still, he could think of nothing.

The summer gradually passed, July turned into August, and nothing happened. No bulldozers came to begin the leveling, no huge pipes were brought for the conduit. And little by little the animals came to believe that if they just refused to think about it, the destruction of the meadow could not take place. That was what Ellen did, too: she simply would not consider it. When she brought the little kids over, she wouldn't even let them talk about it. It is not a very good way to deal with a problem, but when all else fails, people often will not admit to themselves that something truly bad can happen.

So the days went by. Leaves thickened in the light and heat, flowers opened and blossomed beside the brook, the grass in Pasture Land grew smooth—the summer, as always, blessed everything. But hidden somewhere in the sunshine, in the happy chatter of the stream as it ran, there hung a dreadful threat. Ellen and the little kids, and all the animals too, might try to hide their minds from it and pretend it wasn't there —but it was, and it emptied August of all its joy.

There came a morning when a great clanking and clattering was heard on the road. People lined up on both sides to see what was happening—the kids, both big and little, on the side with the houses and the animals from the meadow on the other. Down the street drove a long, flat truck, and on its back a steam shovel was riding. The steam shovel's name— BERTHA—was printed in large letters on one side. The truck stopped at the corner of the meadow, and the two men who ran the steam shovel—their names were Sam and Lou—began driving her down a ramp, off the truck's back, and straight toward the hill above Simon's Pool.

Now, as a rule, steam shovels are very nice. They are wonderful fun to watch while they're working, and they're even more fun to get inside, if the man who is operating one should let you come into the cab. But only the big kids enjoyed watching Bertha work that morning. For she had come to begin the destruction of the meadow.

"Well, it's started," said Chester Cricket.

Tucker Mouse, who was sitting beside him, said nothing at all. He felt as if he had turned to stone. There was nothing he could do but sit there and stare at Bertha Steam Shovel.

When she'd been unloaded, the truck that brought her drove away. And after a while the big kids got tired of watching, and they went off too. The only ones left—on the human side of the road, that is—were the little kids and Ellen. She made them all take hands and led them, with Ruff, across the road. On top of the hill, well out of reach of Bertha's shovel, they stood and silently watched.

The men in the cab saw them standing, motionless, just looking and nothing more, and began to grow uneasy. Sam, who was working the shovel just then, pulled the lever that lowered it to the ground. "Hey, you kids!" he shouted. "What do you want?"

The little kids bunched around Ellen. Jaspar pulled her hand. "Go on!" he pleaded. "You promised, Ellen!"

Ellen detached herself from the hands that were holding on to her and walked to the edge of the gouge the steam shovel had made in the side of the hill. "Mister," she called, "will you do us a favor?"

She was wearing a pair of blue short pants and a blouse with insects pictured on it—butterflies, beetles, and a couple of crickets, too—and she looked very pretty as she asked for her favor. The men in the cab smiled at each other. "Sure, kid!" said Sam. "What is it?"

"Well—um—would you please stop digging up the meadow?" said Ellen. "I mean, as a favor—would you?"

The men looked at each other again, and they were not smiling now. "We have to, kid," said Lou. "The company we work for's been hired to put up apartment buildings here. If it wasn't us that worked ol' Bertha, somebody else would."

"Oh," said Ellen. "Oh. I see." She turned away— then turned back again. "Thanks anyway." And she returned to the little kids on the hill. As before, they stood silent, watching.

The men in the steam shovel talked quietly together. When they spoke out loud, their voices sounded embarrassed and unhappy. "Hey—you kids better get across the street!" said Sam.

"Yeah—we don't want you to get hurt," said Lou.

Ellen made the little kids take hands and took them across to the Hadleys' front lawn. But there they stopped and continued their vigil, staring, without a word, at the steam shovel and the men who ran her. Sam worked the levers, and Bertha took a few more bites out of the hill. Then, since it was almost noon, and since Sam didn't seem to be enjoying his work as much as he usually did, Lou suggested they stop for lunch. They walked over the hill and found a comfortable patch of grass—out of sight of the children. From brown paper bags they took sandwiches and soda pop, and began to eat. Chester and Tucker crept close enough to hear what they were saying.

"I don't blame those kids," said Sam. "When I was that age I used to live next to a swamp. I had this ol' dog—he just wandered into the yard one day an' took a likin' to me an' stayed. Him and me used to go hunt'n' an' fishin' in that swamp.''

"What happened to it?" said Lou.

"They filled it all in an' made a shoppin' center. An' that dog got one look of that shoppin' center, an' he took off. He wasn't stickin' around for any shoppin' center!" Sam put down his sandwich—a meat-loaf sandwich, which his wife knew was his favorite—and looked out over the meadow. Its living green sparkled and glowed below them. "Best time I ever had as a kid was trampin' around that swamp with that dog.''

Lou lay back. Usually he and Sam worked more toward the center of Hedley; all they had to sit down on was a hard, stone curb. But now there was soft, warm grass beneath them. "I don't see why they have to build apartment houses right here anyway," he said. "There's lots of places downtown they could find." He lifted himself up and looked over the hill. "Those kids are gone. They must be havin' lunch too.''

"Don't worry," said Sam, "they'll be back!"

And he was right. As soon as lunch was over, Ellen and the little kids assembled from their various homes and stood at the edge of the Hadleys' yard—and just looked.

"Listen—let's let them sit in the cab," said Sam.

"The boss doesn't like us doin' that," said Lou.

"I don't care what the boss likes!" Sam said angrily. "Here we are, rippin' up the place where those kids play—I know how they feel! Hey, you kids!" he called across the street. "You want to sit in the cab of the steam shovel?"

The children came across the road. Lou lifted them up, one by one, and each sat a minute in the driver's seat, with all the levers in front of them. When Jaspar's turn came, Ruff insisted on climbing up in the cab with him. Lou let him, too. "Turn on the motor!" commanded Jaspar. "I want to work the shovel!"

"Wait a couple of years." Lou laughed. "Maybe then you can."

While the little kids were having their fun in the cab, Sam was talking with Ellen. He asked her what her name was. "Ellen," she answered.

"I'm Sam," he said. "I'm sorry about—about havin' to dig the place up, Ellen. But you can't fight City Hall. The only thing those men on the Town Council pay any mind to is a picket line."

"What's a picket line?" said Ellen. Sam had been on strike a few times and he explained about picket lines: how people marched back and forth carrying signs that said what they thought was wrong with something. It was a way of making everyone pay attention to something that they didn't know, or didn't want to know, or had forgotten. "And if there's a picket line, then—then, can you *change* things?" asked Ellen.

"Sometimes you can," said Sam. "Sometimes not."

Lou had finished lifting the little kids into the cab

and brought them back to Ellen. "Your turn," he said to her.

"Don't bother about me," said Ellen. "I've got something important I have to do this afternoon!" She made the little kids take hands and get ready to cross the road.

"Listen, Ellen," said Sam. "Would you do *me* a favor now? Would you all please stop starin' at us? It gets under our skin—you know?"

"I'm sorry," said Ellen. "We won't watch you any more." She told the little kids to say thank you—which they did, one by one, Nancy, Anne, John, and last Jaspar—and quickly took them back to the houses. They wanted to stay with her, but she sent them off to play hide-and-seek and then hurried home to take care of her own important business.

Sam watched her go. "Nice kid," he said.

"They're all nice," said Lou.

Sam was silent for a while. Then he said, "Listen— I'm goin' to take out Bertha's spark plugs."

"You're *what?*" said Lou.

"Bertha's gett'n' old," said Sam. He patted the steam shovel's side. "She has a right to a breakdown."

"Boy, are you goin' crazy!" said Lou. "The boss'll—"

"Forget about the boss!" Sam interrupted. He looked at Lou sharply. "You aren't goin' to tell him, are you?"

"Course not!" said Lou. Sam stepped up into the cab

and opened the door to the motor's compartment. He unscrewed two little things and put them in his pocket. "It won't do any good," said Lou. "She'll be outa commission this afternoon, but they'll fix her by tomorrow."

"That's right," said Sam. "But at least this afternoon we won't have to dig up this hill." He gave the big caterpillar tread of the steam shovel another friendly pat. "You take a rest, ol' girl!"

And Lou and he walked down the road, toward the corner where a larger avenue crossed it. They could get a bus there downtown.

For a minute the hill seemed deserted. It wasn't, however. Tucker Mouse and Chester Cricket crept out from the bushes where they'd been hiding. "Those men are nice," said Tucker.

"Most people are," said the cricket. "If they just get left alone. It's when they all get together that they start doing stupid things—like digging up meadows!"

Tucker looked at the steam shovel towering above them. "Um—Chester—I know Bertha shouldn't be here, but as long as she is—um—"

"Go ahead," said Chester. "Go sit in the cab if you want to."

"You wouldn't think I'm joining the enemy, would you?"

"No, no," said the cricket. "Go on."

The mouse scrambled up over the tread and into

the cab. He made his way up, gear by gear, until he was sitting in the driver's seat. It occurred to him that he might be the only mouse in the world who had ever sat in the driver's seat of a steam shovel. But, under the circumstances, the thought didn't make him very happy.

NINE

The Picket Line

Early next day Chester and Tucker were down beside the brook next to the stump, having their morning wash and drink. Their backs were toward the bank. "Good morning," said a voice behind them. They both looked up, and there sat Harry Cat.

"What are you doing here?" said Tucker.

"Ellen and the little kids are out in the meadow," Harry answered.

"So early?" said Chester.

"Yes," said Harry. "Come on. I want you to see something."

Tucker knew that something was wrong. Harry Cat had a way of flicking his tail to right and to left when he was upset or angry, and right now his tail was lashing like a whip. "What's the matter, Harry?" said the mouse.

"You'll see," said Harry. "Just come on."

No one spoke as they walked through Tuffet Coun-

try and Pasture Land. When they got to the foot of
the hill, Tucker could see what was wrong. Up on top
of it there was a picket line. Ellen and the little kids
were marching around in a circle. Each one of them
was carrying a sign, and they were marching right next
to the hole the steam shovel had made yesterday, so
that everyone could tell exactly what the signs referred
to. Ellen's sign said LET THE MEADOW ALONE. Nancy was
carrying one with STOP BUILDING printed on it. Anne
was holding up a sign almost as big as she was herself.
It read DOWN WITH HOUSES. John was the little kid who
most liked to sit beside the water and just look at the
fishes and frogs and things. His sign said HELP THE
BROOK. And Jaspar had demanded to carry the sign
printed in the biggest letters of all: SAVE NATURE!

"Ellen spent all yesterday afternoon making those
signs," said Harry. "That's the third set. She decided
the letters in the first two weren't big enough. And she
also made those poles that the cardboard's attached to.
She hammered them together out of that wood we saw
in the cellar." Harry was speaking in a very flat voice.
But Tucker knew there was stony anger inside him.
"She got three splinters, too. Her mother had to take
them out with a needle."

The three animals looked at the children on the hill,
marching in their picket line. "I *hate* Connecticut!"
Chester Cricket burst out.

"Chester!" said Tucker Mouse in amazement. "*You*

say you hate Connecticut? The way you love it—?"

"I don't care!" said the cricket. "It's *not right* when kids have to do things like that!"

"The mothers think so, too," said Harry. He led the mouse and the cricket up the side of the hill.

On the other side of the road a little crowd had gathered. The mothers of the little kids were standing with Mrs. Hadley at the edge of the Hadleys' front yard. Some big kids were there too, sitting on the grass. David, Jaspar's brother, was fourteen years old, and he was definitely a big kid. He had taken a course in civics the year before in school, and he was very proud of all he knew about society. "Hey, Jaspar!" he shouted. "Who's your union leader?"

Jaspar didn't understand that he was being laughed at. "Ellen Hadley!" he called back happily.

David looked at his and Jaspar's mother. "I think that's a dopey thing to do!" he scoffed. "Marching around like that."

But his mother cut him off with a glance. "Be quiet, David," she said softly. And sometimes the softness in a mother's voice can be much worse than her loudness is.

The big kids hung around a little longer—then they went off to play by themselves. But the mothers stayed on. Mothers do, when things like this happen. "Do you suppose they *have* to put up apartment houses right here?" said Anne's mother.

John's mother shifted uneasily. "I suppose that's what they call 'progress.'"

"I don't call it progress!" exploded Jaspar's mother furiously. "I call it a *shame!*" Jaspar took after his mother in many ways.

Ruff Saint Bernard, who happened to be sitting nearby, scratching one ear, caught the mood of the mothers and began to bark furiously. Jaspar's mother shushed him. "*That* won't do any good!" she said. Ruff gave one last frustrated 'woof!' and went back to scratching his ear.

"I think I'll make some lemonade for everybody," said Nancy's mother. She went off toward her own home, which was next door to the Hadleys': a brick house with red shutters.

"You know what we ought to do?" said Mrs. Hadley. "We ought to take those signs ourselves and go down and march around City Hall!"

"Yes, we really should," said John's mother. "But I've got such a tubful of laundry to do this afternoon—"

"—and there's the marketing for the whole weekend." Anne's mother sighed and shook her head.

The mothers stood silent, thinking of what they ought to do and of all the little, necessary chores that would keep them from doing it. In a few minutes Nancy's mother came back with a big pitcher of lemonade and some paper cups. The five women crossed the road. Tucker Mouse, who had one encounter with Mrs. Hadley already, was careful to stay out of sight.

"How about some lemonade?" said Nancy's mother cheerfully.

"We don't have time," said Ellen.

"No time!" said Jaspar sternly.

"Oh, just for a *minute* you could stop," said Anne's mother.

The sweat was standing out in beads on John's forehead. He wiped them off and said hopefully, "It *is* getting hot, Ellen—"

"All right," said Ellen. "But everybody keep your signs pointing toward the road."

"I wouldn't mind a slug of lemonade myself," Tucker whispered to Chester.

Nancy's mother poured out lemonade for all the children. Picketing in August is very hot work, and it tasted delicious.

"Ellen," said Mrs. Hadley, "I know how you feel about the meadow, and keeping it the way it is, but— do you really think this marching will do any good?"

"Well, it could," said Ellen. "We ought to go and march where the Town Council meets, but I can't take the little kids way downtown." The mothers glanced at one another, but their eyes didn't like to meet. "And I was hoping," Ellen went on, "that people who drive by here would see us. And then *they'd* go downtown and tell everybody we were marching. And if enough people did it—well, maybe they wouldn't dig up the meadow." She looked from one mother to another. "Isn't that possible?"

"It's possible," said Mrs. Hadley without much hope, "but—"

"That's all it has to be," said Ellen. "Just possible. Thank you for the lemonade. Everybody in line now!" She marshaled the little kids again. "And hold your signs so the people in cars can see."

Nancy's mother held up the pitcher. "I think there's probably going to be a steady supply of lemonade in my kitchen today. Anybody who gets thirsty—just come over."

"Oh boy!" said Jaspar. He looked at Ellen, and then back at Nancy's mother, and said firmly, "I mean—no time!" And the picket line began its march again.

Jaspar's mother shook her head. "The least we can do is to make sure that this is the best Hedley Day the children have ever had."

"Good heavens! Is it time for Hedley Day already?" said John's mother. "How the summer flies!"

Ellen's mother looked out across the meadow. "This is the last year we'll be able to have the picnic here." Her eyes traced the rambling course of the brook. "It does seem a pity."

All the mothers agreed that it was a pity. Then they returned to their separate homes and began the necessary little chores that filled up ordinary days.

The Picket Line

"It's Friday today," said Ellen to the little kids as they marched in their circle. "If we picket today and tomorrow and Hedley Day too, a lot of people are *sure* to see us!"

"What's 'Hedley Day'?" whispered Tucker to Chester Cricket.

"The last Sunday in August is Hedley Day," Chester told him. "All around town everybody has picnics and makes speeches. It's in honor of that man, Joseph Hedley."

"Was it his birthday?" asked Tucker.

"No," said the cricket. "That is, I guess it might have been. No one knows just which day he was born. They don't even know where he lived, exactly. But he was so important that they have a celebration anyway. I think most folks enjoy the food more than the speeches. The kids do, at least. But everyone seems to have a good time. In this neighborhood the mothers divide up who makes what to eat, and if the weather's nice, they have the picnic in the meadow."

By now the morning was well along. For a while the three animals sat and watched the picket march in silence. Then Tucker Mouse sighed and said, "I wish I was big enough to carry a sign."

"I know what it would say," said Harry Cat. "BE-WARE! FEROCIOUS MOUSE! THIS MEANS YOU!"

Just then a dump truck pulled up beside the road. It was brand new and painted a bright green. The man driving it was named Frank. Sitting beside him in the front seat were Sam and Lou. They both got out, and Frank grinned at them through the open window. He thought it was much more important work to drive a brand-new dump truck than to run a rickety old steam shovel. "Now remember what the boss said, boys," he called. "If Bertha needs two new spark plugs today, she's going to need two new guys to work her!"

"Yeah!" muttered Lou.

"Wise guy!" growled Sam. He and Lou climbed the hill and saw the picket line. They stopped, and for a moment stood frozen. Sam's face went tight, as if he was trying not to see what he saw.

"Hi," said Ellen. She thought the men were angry with her, and tried to apologize. "We're not doing anything wrong. Honestly!"

"I know you're not, honey," said Sam. "But you've got to go back to your own yard now. Lou an' me are in big trouble. We have to do two days' work today— to make up for yesterday afternoon. Go on now." He touched Ellen's shoulder. She made the little kids take hands. "And Ellen—I really am—" Sam was about to say "sorry," but the word felt so empty in his mind that he didn't even want to hear himself say it. Ellen took the signs under one arm and led the little kids across the road.

All day Bertha worked—without stopping for the noon hour even. First Lou had her dig up the pile

The Picket Line

of dirt left from yesterday morning and lift it into the dump truck. Frank drove it over to another part of town where a site was being filled in for a factory. Then, when Sam began his turn, he made her bite into the living ground. By the time the men left, late Friday afternoon, half the hill had been eaten away.

On the other side of the street, at the edge of the Hadleys' lawn, the picket line went on. There were two or three breaks for lemonade, and a longer stop for lunch, but the children marched until six o'clock. The mothers were amazed. Usually little kids like to change their games often, but on this particular summer day no one, not even Jaspar, suggested that they do anything else—because this was not a game. At suppertime, however, the mothers insisted that the picket line be disbanded—temporarily, at least. And as a matter of fact, suppers were especially good in the neighborhood that night; many favorite dishes were served. But before she had her dinner, Ellen stored the signs in the Hadleys' garage, where they'd be waiting for tomorrow.

All during the day the usual stream of cars had flowed along the road. Quite a few of the drivers slowed down to watch the picket line. Some shook their heads, some only stared in amazement. And no one laughed. But no one went down to the City Hall either, to tell the Town Council that children with signs were marching beside the Old Meadow.

At dusk, when the children and the workmen had

gone, the animals gathered beside the steep hollow that gaped in the side of the hill. Bill Squirrel was there, and Henry Chipmunk, and so were various rabbits and sundry fieldmice. The roots of the elm tree where Bill had his nest had just begun to show. "One more day," said Bill. "That's all it'll take."

Tucker Mouse wished that it was already dark so he couldn't see the others and nobody could see him. "I'm a failure," he said. "I failed. I couldn't think of anything."

"It's not your fault," said Chester. "I guess there are some things you just can't stop."

The animals sat on the verge of the pit, and the August night came on.

TEN

Henry's House

"I wish you'd come, Mr. Mouse. I really do!"

It was Saturday morning. Chester and Tucker and several of the other animals were sitting on the hill watching Ellen and the little kids picket. The children had gotten up just as early today as they had yesterday, and right after breakfast they were out on the Hadleys' lawn, marching around in the same circle.

"Please come, Mr. Mouse." Henry Chipmunk was talking. "I've been asking you and Mr. Cat to come and visit me and Emily at our house all summer long. And by next week we won't *have* any house! It's really very interesting, where we live. You'll enjoy it!" A forlorn expression came over the chipmunk's face. "And if you don't come, Emily's going to think you don't like us."

Harry Cat had come over to join his friends. "Come on, Tucker," he said. "We can't have Emily thinking that."

"All right." Tucker sighed. He could not take his

eyes off the marching children. "But I wish there was some way I could help those kids. Maybe if I threw myself in front of the next car that comes—"

"What kind of help would that be?" said Chester.

"Well, the car might stop, and Ellen could tell the driver what they're doing, and—"

"Come on." Harry gently prodded the mouse. "Let's go see where Henry and Emily live."

With Chester hopping along beside them, the animals went down the hill, walked around Simon's Pool, past Ellen's Special Place, and came to a spot where a big log was caught against the bank of the brook. It projected out into the water, and from the end of it an easy jump could be made to the farther bank. When everyone was on the other side, Tucker Mouse looked back. The morning sun made a golden picture that knitted together the birches of Ellen's Special Place, the glittering surface of Simon's Pool, and the hill above, where Bill Squirrel's elm was growing. The yawning cavity on the other side could not be seen— only the steam shovel's roof. But since it was Saturday, Bertha would not be working today.

Tucker shook his head. "To think of everything— just gone!"

"Don't think of it," said Chester.

Henry Chipmunk led them off toward the West, through land that was very much like Pasture Land: flat grass with daisies and buttercups and low, blue forget-me-nots growing in it. On any other day it would have been a happy parade that tramped through the fields, surrounded by flowers. Soon the ground began to rise, and they came to a hilly country where tangled old trees were planted in rows. "These are apple trees," Henry explained. "Ages ago, when there used to be a farm here, the farmer had an orchard. You should smell how sweet it smells in the fall, when all the apples are lying on the ground!"

Beyond the orchard there was an open space, and then two great oak trees loomed up before them. "This used to be the farm's front yard," said Henry. "Emily and I live just past those oak trees."

The animals walked between the trees—like passing through a huge, natural doorway—and came to a big hole in the ground. The sides had fallen in, especially the west side, opposite them, but they could see that the excavation must once have been square. "That's a pretty big hole for a little chipmunk like you!" said Tucker.

"Oh, that's not our house!" Henry laughed. "That's the cellar of the old farm house. Here's where *we* live!"

At one corner of the cellar grew a large clump of lilac bushes. Emily was sitting under them waiting for her guests. Good mornings were said all around, and then Emily led the way down a ledge where the dirt from one wall had collapsed. A few feet from the top a nice, dry little cave opened out on the left. And this was Henry and Emily's home. The animals all went in—except Harry. He was too big to fit in comfortably, so he sat on the ledge outside.

Emily had been expecting Tucker and Harry all summer long, and in order to give them something to eat she'd been saving fruit from the ruins on the farm's back-yard kitchen garden. First she'd saved strawberries; then, when they went out of season, raspberries; then blueberries; and now she was all the way up to peaches. It wasn't easy for the little chipmunk to wrestle a peach all the way around the cellar, down the ledge, and into her house—but she'd managed somehow. Very politely, and proudly too, she offered everyone some fruit. And naturally they all accepted.

"I wish you'd been able to come and visit us in the early spring, Mr. Mouse," she said to Tucker. "The lilacs are beautiful when they're in bloom! The biggest bush up there is the deepest purple—you just can't imagine!" Emily was silent a moment, thinking about her favorite lilac. "When the meadow's—I mean, when we're not living here any more, it's going to be the lilacs that I miss most."

An awkward pause fell. To break it Harry Cat switched his tail and said, "Tucker, you should see what's down in that cellar. It's almost as cluttered as the Hadleys' attic."

Tucker crept out to the edge of the ledge. At first all he could see was the jumble of thickets and bushes that had taken root on the floor of the cellar. Then his eyes picked out what looked like fragments of furniture and the glint of broken glass. "Say, that's very interesting!" he said. "Emily, would you mind if I went down and scrounged awhile? It's been so long!"

"Go right ahead," said the chipmunk.

"I'm going, too!" said Henry.

"You be careful, Henry," his sister warned.

Chester stayed in the cave to talk to Emily, but Tucker, Harry, and Henry walked around the rim of the cellar to the west side where it was easier to descend. They scrambled and stumbled and tumbled their way until they were down on the cellar floor. Then began the delightful business of exploring in a ruin.

"That farm house must have been very old," said Harry. "See this piece of glass? Those wavy lines in it are flaws. In the old days they didn't know how to make glass as well as they do now." In his travels in New York, Harry had browsed through several antique shops, and he knew a lot about things like old glass.

"I think the whole place must have burned down," said Henry. He had discovered the wreckage of an ancient wooden rocking chair. What was left of one arm was blackened and charred.

But Tucker made the most interesting discovery. He was burrowing under a wild rose bush that had taken root amid the rubble, and he came on the re-

mains of a huge book of some kind. "Hey, come here!"
he called to the others. Henry and Harry came over,
and together all three hauled and pulled and managed
to lift the book's cover. The page underneath was
browned and half eaten away, as if it, too, had been
burned by fire. And of course it had been soaked by
the rains and snows of many years. But there was writ-
ing on that page, and it still was barely legible.

Harry Cat read the words: *Family Bible of Joseph
Henry*.

"He must have been the man who owned the farm!"
exclaimed Henry.

"And he went off and left his family Bible," said
Tucker. "Can you beat that!"

"He probably thought it got burned in the fire,"
said Harry.

They rummaged through the cellar for an hour or
so. With the bushes and wild flowers growing amid
the remains of things that had once been inside the
farm house, it was like being indoors and outdoors at
the same time—a funny feeling. Then Emily called
down and said that Chester thought it was time to be
going. The west bank was steeper than the three explorers had realized, however, and climbing up was
much harder than coming down. Harry had to boost
Tucker and Henry over the rim. But at last they were
on level ground again.

Chester and Emily were waiting under the lilacs.

"Did you have a nice time, Mr. Mouse?" asked the chipmunk.

"A very fine time," said Tucker. "It's excellent scrounging ground down there!" He looked back into the cellar, at the jumble of old, lost human things that nature had reclaimed. "Fascinating, in fact!"

The others began to say goodbye, but Tucker continued gazing downward. His whiskers started to twitch, and he muttered something to himself.

"What did you say?" said Harry Cat.

"I didn't say anything," said the mouse.

"Yes, you did," said Harry.

"Oh, I was just thinking out loud," said Tucker. "Joseph Henry, Joseph Hedley, Ellen Hadley. Hmm." His whiskers were wiggling furiously—always a good sign. "Chester, that important man, Hedley, his first name *was* Joseph, wasn't it?"

"Yes," said Chester. "Why?"

"No reason," said Tucker. "And no one knows where he lived. Hmm."

No one spoke. Then Harry said softly, "Tucker— what are you thinking?"

"I don't know what I'm thinking," said Tucker Mouse. "But I'm thinking something. I've got to find out what it is." He walked off by himself and began pacing back and forth.

"Do you think—" Chester started to speak.

But Harry lifted one paw. "Shh."

The two chipmunks, the cat, and the cricket sat silent. Tucker Mouse had stopped his pacing and was pointing before him at something which wasn't there. Then he pointed at something else, which also wasn't there. And then, with a shout—*"I got it!"*—he jumped three feet straight up.

"I got it! I got it!" He came running back to the others.

In one voice Emily, Henry, Chester, and Harry all exclaimed, *"What?"*

"No time to tell you now!" said Tucker Mouse. "Call all the animals! Everybody in the meadow! Pheasants, squirrels! The various and sundries, too! Get them all together down by Simon's Pool! As fast as you can! I'll explain it to everyone then! We've only got a single day! But the Old Meadow is saved!" He looked down into the cellar, eyes wide with excitement but shadowed by a bit of doubt. "At least maybe it's saved—I hope!"

ELEVEN

How to Build a Discovery

Like a wind, word spread through the meadow that the mouse from New York had another plan. From all quarters, animals streamed toward Simon's Pool. By noon a great crowd had collected around the log where the old turtle sunned himself. He was lying there now, waiting like the others to hear what Tucker had to say. The mouse jumped up on the log beside him and looked out over the upturned, expectant faces before him.

"Friends and meadow dwellers!" he began. "As you know, the ripping up of your home has already begun." A groan went up from the assembly. "Those humans should only have known better!" said Tucker. "But just this morning I came down with an idea that still might work!"

"Hooray!" came a cry from the section where the sundry fieldmice were sitting.

"Save the 'hoorays' till we're safe!" said Tucker. He went on to explain what had happened. "Just a little while ago we discovered that the farm house where

Henry and Emily live had been the home of a man
named Joseph Henry, and *I* got the idea that—"

"Joseph Henry!" exclaimed Simon Turtle. "Why,
I haven't heard that name for—for—goodness, I can't
even recollect how many years!"

"Very interesting, Mr. Turtle," said Tucker, who
was anxious to get on with his plan, "however, right
now—"

But Simon had begun one of his reminiscences—an especially interesting one, to him, because it brought back a scene he hadn't remembered for ages. "I recollect my grandfather—Amos Turtle was his name—and I recollect him telling me when I was just out of the egg that *his* grandfather—that would be my great-*great*-grandfather—"

125

"Mr. Turtle—!" Tucker began tapping his foot.

"—*his* grandfather," Simon went right on, "had told *my* grandfather that he remembered the days when the Henry family was still living in that farm house. He told him about the night of the fire. I recollect my grandfather saying that the Henrys used to have an old dog, and the dog knocked over a kerosene lamp— way back in those times, before electricity, they used kerosene—and—"

"*Mr. Turtle!*" Tucker Mouse burst out impatiently. "If you'll let me tell you about my plan, and if my plan *does* work, maybe *your* grandchildren will have something to recollect, too!"

Tucker's indignation shocked Simon out of his reveries back into the present. "Oh, by all means," he said, "do go on."

"To be brief," said Tucker, with a stern look at the turtle, "what we have to do is convince the human beings that that farm house originally belonged to Joseph Hedley, not Joseph Henry. You said that the human beings didn't know exactly where Joseph Hedley lived, didn't you, Chester?"

"Yes, I did," said the cricket, "but—"

"Wait." The mouse held up one claw. "If we can get the human beings believing that the Old Meadow was the location of the Joseph Hedley homestead and farm, *my* guess is that they won't dare wreck a place of such—" His squeaky voice became very grand and im-

portant. "—such historical significance! So we've just got to fool the stupid human beings. How about it? What do you think?"

The animals all looked at one another, testing the idea in their minds. Then a few began to smile, and a few more began to laugh. A wave of excitement and enthusiasm broke over them. To fool the human beings would be a game, as well as a means of saving the Old Meadow.

"Here's how I think we can do it," said Tucker. "First we—"

"Uh—Tucker," said Chester Cricket, "excuse me for interrupting you. But even if we *can* do it, wouldn't it be sort of—well, I mean, like a lie?"

"Oh, *Chester!*" Tucker shouted. "You're so honorable! It's disgusting! Here the human beings are about to ruin your home! Everybody's home! And you're worrying about telling a little lie! The only other thing I can think of to do is wait until Monday morning, and then have all of us who have teeth big enough go out there and attack those workmen! We might get the town believing the meadow was full of rabid rodents. But they'd probably just come out here and exterminate us anyway!"

"Chester," said Harry Cat, "just keep telling yourself it's not a lie—it's a benign deception. For everybody's good."

"That's right!" said Tucker. "A 'benign deception.'"

For everybody's good! The human beings' good, too—
if they don't have brains enough to leave nice meadows
alone!" Another idea struck him. "And imagine the
noble sentiments, Chester! How proud they'll all be—
to have discovered the Joseph Hedley homestead. I
could weep to think of the patriotism!"

"Well—" began Chester.

"Fine! That's settled!" said Tucker Mouse. "Here's
what we do: first of all, the various and the sundries
have to ransack that cellar hunting for things that don't
look old—*very* old! If you have any doubts—about
dishes, say, or furniture—ask either Harry or Chester
or me. But anything that doesn't look at least a couple
of hundred years old—drag it out of the cellar and
hide it somewhere! Hop to it now, you rabbits and
mousiekins!" Tucker was really getting in the spirit
of things; he clapped his paws and rubbed them together like the foreman of a crew. The various rabbits
and sundry fieldmice dashed off toward the ruins of
the farm house.

"We'd like to help, too," said a cultured voice from
one side. Beatrice and Jerome Pheasant had been sitting a little apart from the others.

"Great!" said Tucker. "You two go with the various
and the sundries. And *scrounge,* Beatrice! Scrounge
like you never scrounged before!"

Beatrice Pheasant looked a little shocked on receiv-

ing these instructions. Needless to say, she had never "scrounged" before in her life. And she didn't relish the idea of spending the day in the company of a crowd of ordinary fieldmice. But she realized that this was an emergency, so she swallowed her pride—and told Jerome to swallow his, too—and off they fluttered. As a matter of fact, by late afternoon she found that she rather enjoyed this "scrounging"—or "antiquing," as she preferred to call it. It was she who uncovered a solid silver spoon. Everyone thought that a solid silver spoon was exactly right for the Joseph Hedley homestead. But then Beatrice, with her sharp pheasant eyes, noticed that down at the end of the handle there was printed in tiny figures the date when the spoon had been made: 1834. It was decided that 1834 was far too recent a year for Joseph Hedley to have owned the spoon. Beatrice said that in that case she would like to have it herself, and she took it back to her nest. The other things that were too new—a Campbell's soup can, for instance— were carted off and buried in the orchard.

While work went on in the cellar, Tucker Mouse was still issuing commands beside Simon's Pool. "Now the most important thing—and this is a job for you, Harry—is to get that sign we saw in the Hadleys' attic. Remember that sign we saw, that had HADLEY stamped on it in iron letters? I have to have it! It's the key to everything!"

"I can help you there," said Bill Squirrel. "There's a hole under the eaves of the Hadleys' roof big enough for two squirrels to march in abreast. And we have, too! There's more that goes on in those attics than the human beings know about."

"Wonderful!" said Tucker. "Then you help Harry. But wait till the Hadleys have gone to sleep—it'll be easier then."

"Hadley's not the same as Hedley," said Harry Cat.

"Never you mind," Tucker silenced him. "Just you watch what I'm going to do! And don't let me forget that I've got to chew off part of the first page of Joseph Henry's family Bible."

"What are you going to do that for?" said Harry. "That ought to be lugged away, too. It's a sure give-away."

"Not when I get through with it, it won't be!" said Tucker. "I'm going to doctor it up so it reads *Family Bible of Joseph He*—and then the page ends. The human beings'll think the *He*— stands for Hedley. And what could be more precious to the town of Hedley than the family Bible of Joseph Hedley himself? Hic! hic! hic!" He couldn't contain himself and burst into a series of squeaky laughs. "You shouldn't be upset, Chester—it's just another little benign deception."

Chester couldn't help but laugh himself. He shook his head. "You've got to admit it—when Tucker works at something, he really *works* at it!"

How to Build a Discovery

Tucker Mouse gave a superior little sniff. "You said it!" he agreed. "This is one mousiekins with imagination!"

Ellen and the little kids continued to picket almost all the afternoon. They didn't know it, but on this particular Saturday they weren't the only ones who were working to save the Old Meadow. In the ruined orchard, through the portal oaks, and down inside the farm-house cellar there was a bustling of activity such as the meadow had not seen for years. Fieldmice were chewing up an old canvas suitcase. Chester said it could stay in the cellar, but only if it looked more torn and shredded. Rabbits were scratching up a set of wooden bowls. They had aged very nicely and been partly burned in the fire, too—exactly the kind of clues Tucker wanted. Beatrice and Jerome Pheasant, having appropriated the silver spoon, were now sifting through a pile of broken glass, picking out the most weathered pieces and flying the rest over to a hole Henry Chipmunk had dug on the far side of the orchard.

And Tucker Mouse was running around everywhere, shouting encouragement. "Remember! It has to be all finished by picnic time tomorrow! Hedley Day is the only time when lots of human beings come to the meadow, isn't it, Chester?"

"Yes," said the cricket. "And besides, if this doesn't work tomorrow, by next week it'll be too late anyway."

Tucker's Countryside

Tucker kept looking into the west and wishing the sun would go down. "I've got to get that sign!" he said. When night finally did come, he and Bill Squirrel and Chester went back to the hill and waited for the lights in the Hadleys' house to go out. Work didn't stop in the cellar, however. There was a full moon for the animals to see by, and the sifting and searching went on all night.

It was a habit of Mrs. and Mr. Hadley to sit up late on Saturday nights and watch a movie on television. On this night the movie was one of their favorites. They had seen it years ago, even before Ellen was born, and it was like being young again to see it once more together. They enjoyed it very much.

Tucker Mouse did not enjoy it, though. By midnight he was bouncing around like a rubber ball. "What are those people?" he demanded impatiently. "Human beings or night owls?"

"Harry must be getting awfully nervous, too," said Chester.

"Mmm," grumbled Tucker. "He's been living over there like a king all summer—now let him do his duty for once!"

"There it goes!" said Bill Squirrel. The light in the master bedroom had just winked out. "Now is that sign all you want? What if I find something else that looks really old?"

"*Steal it!*" said Tucker happily. Then, to ease the

cricket's conscience, he added, "Now now, now now—
just grit your teeth, Chester. Win or lose, it'll all be
over tomorrow."

Bill darted across the road, up the Hadleys' lawn,
and flickered up a maple tree that grew in front of the
house. Its branches overhung the roof, and in a second
he was inside the attic. Harry Cat was waiting for him.
He pointed to the sign. In the dim moonlight that
entered through a narrow window the iron letters—
HADLEY—stood out. Without a word, the squirrel and
the cat began dragging it to the hole where Bill had
entered.

That part of the attic was just above Mr. and Mrs.
Hadley's bedroom. Mrs. Hadley sat up in bed. "Dear,"
she said, "I hear something in the attic."

"What?" mumbled Mr. Hadley, who was half asleep.

"I don't know," said Mrs. Hadley. "But I've told you
a dozen times I think squirrels are getting in up there."

"I'll look into it tomorrow," said Mr. Hadley into
his pillow.

"It's not the first time I've heard *that*," said Mrs.
Hadley. She rolled over and went to sleep.

Bill and Harry pulled and hauled the sign to the
hole under the eaves of the roof. "Better just push it
out," the squirrel whispered. They counted three and
heaved. Down fell the sign, missing the flagstone front
walk, on which it would have made an awful clatter,
by a couple of inches. It dropped, with a soft thud, on

the grass. Harry decided that it was easier to follow Bill Squirrel than go down the stairs inside the house, so he too climbed out the hole, over the gutter, and onto the roof. "Kind of like housebreaking, isn't it?" Bill laughed in the darkness. They both jumped up to the branch of the maple tree and made their way down to the lawn. From there it was no problem to lug the sign across the road.

"About time!" said Tucker Mouse when he saw the two of them emerging from the night.

"I'm going back and look for some old things now," said Bill. Before Chester could say that he thought they had enough, he had vanished back toward the Hadleys'.

"Well, here's the sign," said Harry. "What are we going to do with it?"

"*This* is what I'm going to do!" said Tucker. He began chewing furiously at the wood around the letter A.

"You'll get splinters in your tongue," said Chester.

Tucker spit out a mouthful of wood. "I don't care *where* I get splinters—as long as this plan of mine works!" He resumed his chewing. The nail that held the letter in the wood was deeper than he had thought it would be. It took almost an hour to get it loose. Then Tucker and Harry each took an end of the letter and pushed it and pulled it until they had rocked the A out.

"But look," said Harry. The shape of the A was

clearly pressed into the wood where it had been. "It still looks like HADLEY, but with one letter missing."

"Nothing unexpected," said Tucker confidently. "Don't worry."

Just then Bill Squirrel came back. In one claw he was carrying a colored glass necklace and in the other a pair of plastic earrings with tiny copper beads in them. "Guess what I found!" he exclaimed proudly. "A box of Mrs. Hadley's jewels!"

"*Jewels—*" said Chester in dismay. "Now that really is going too far!"

Tucker Mouse, who had collected some lost jewelry himself in the Times Square subway station, trotted over to have a look. After a preliminary examination he said disappointedly, "It's only costume jewelry. Kind of pretty, though."

Harry Cat switched his tail back and forth. "Somehow," he said softly, "I don't quite think that a glass necklace or a pair of plastic earrings are what you'd expect to find in a pioneer's homestead."

"Hmm." Tucker brooded on that a minute. "I tell you what. If my plan succeeds, I'm sure to deserve a reward. I'll keep the necklace, and you can give the earrings to Beatrice Pheasant. She's starting a collection, too. And if she keeps on scrounging the way she did today, she's going to end up as good as me!"

Chester Cricket sighed and decided not even to *think* of words like "burglary" until tomorrow night.

"Well—back to work!" said Tucker. He started on the sign again—not chewing now, but nibbling at the wood where the letter A had been nailed. Before long, the impression of the A had been completely erased. Tucker spit out the bits of wood and took a deep breath. "Now for the most important part." Very carefully he nibbled a bar that went straight up and down on the sign. Then, off that bar, he nibbled three shorter, parallel bars. The shape of a perfect capital letter E appeared.

"I get it!" said Bill. "They'll think the sign said HEDLEY, but the E dropped out!"

"Right!" said Tucker. "And now, just to make it look *really* old—" He chewed away the wood around the L, until the iron letter came loose. "I don't want this one to come off," said the mouse. "Only be wobbly with age." He stood back and squinted at the sign, like a painter appraising his masterpiece. "Hmm. Still something wrong. It's the sides." Two elegant scroll-like curves were carved into the wood at the ends of the sign, the kind of detail that people in Connecticut like. "Too fancy for a pioneer. Bill, you take that side and I'll do this." The squirrel and the mouse did a few minutes of vigorous chomping. And now the sign really did seem like the wrecked and weathered relic of a bygone age. "There!" said Tucker. "Finished! How's that for a 'benign deception'?"

"Very good!" said Harry Cat. "As a forgery it's not bad either."

How to Build a Discovery

A groan was heard from Chester Cricket.

The animals dragged the sign down the hill, dunked it in Simon's Pool to wash off the chips and also give it the feeling of having been out in the rain and the wet all those years, and then carried it up to the farm-house cellar. The last of the exhausted sundries were just crawling home.

Tucker insisted on going down into the cellar to arrange the sign properly. First he tried it here, then there, then way over there, then back here—but he couldn't be satisfied. "For goodness' sake!" said Harry Cat. "You're not decorating a castle!"

"I know," said Tucker. "I'm furnishing a ruin. But it has to be just right." He finally decided that behind the rosebush was the proper place. That was near enough to the Bible so that they could be found to-gether, but not too near to arouse suspicion. His last bit of nibbling, just as dawn was beginning to break, was to snip off neatly the last three letters of Joseph Henry's name. In the pale, growing light the mouse looked around him. "Well," he asked, "does this look like the ruins of a pioneer's homestead—or doesn't it?"

"I don't know," said Harry. "I've never been in one."

"Anyway," sighed Tucker Mouse, "after all the work I've done tonight, I feel like the ruins of a pioneer!"

TWELVE

Hedley Day

The weather on Sunday was clear and bright and a little brisk—not really summer weather at all, but one of those September days that drop in unexpectedly early, in August. It was a fine day for a picnic, however, and toward noon the families of the neighborhood began coming over into the meadow. Some had folding chairs and tables, and others, who wanted to feel the good ground beneath them, brought only comfortable blankets to sit on. One thing they all had, though, and that was bulging picnic baskets.

Tucker Mouse was sitting up in the hills, with the other animals, amid the trees of the old orchard. They were waiting to see who would be first to discover the ruins of what they now all solemnly spoke of as "the Joseph Hedley homestead." But the sight of those picnic baskets drove every thought but one out of Tucker's mind. "Chester," he said, "I was wondering —the humans being what they are, and wasting so much, there's bound to be a lot of food scattered around—and I was thinking, after they go home, maybe we could have a picnic ourselves—on what they leave."

"If you want to," said Chester. "But honestly, at a time like this I can't think about food."

Tucker asked himself if there could ever be a time when *he* couldn't think about food. He decided it was simply out of the question, but in deference to Chester's feelings he kept quiet anyway.

By one o'clock all the families had arrived. From the hills where the animals were watching them, they made a pretty sight, scattered through the fields below. Everyone was wearing bright summer clothes, but most had brought sweaters because of the coolness in the air. With its members all gathered together, each separate family looked like a different cluster of flowers.

"I wish somebody would come up," said Henry Chipmunk.

"So do I," said Chester.

Tucker Mouse began to fidget. He had caught the smell of broiling meat and had about decided to creep down and see if he couldn't scrounge up a shred of coleslaw or something. But before he could leave, Harry Cat came strolling up. After they'd put the sign in the cellar, Harry had gone back to the Hadleys' house so he'd be there, just as usual, when the family woke up. "Nobody's discovered the homestead yet?" he asked.

"No," said Chester nervously.

"What's that on your whiskers?" said Tucker.

Harry licked off his whiskers. "Ketchup. Mr. Hadley's cooking hamburgers. It's one of Ellen's favorites—"

"It's one of mine, too!" muttered Tucker.

"—and they want her to have a good time. She isn't, though. She's not hungry at all. She said she'd rather picket. But Mrs. Hadley told her that *everybody,* even pickets, have to have one day off."

"So how many hamburgers did you have, Harry?" asked Tucker gloomily.

"Just the half that Ellen couldn't finish," said Harry.

"You *do* think that somebody'll find the things, don't you, Harry?" said Chester.

"I don't see why not," said Harry.

"You know—" Henry began to speak, but then stopped. "Well—I'm not saying it'll happen today—but sometimes the mothers tell the kids not to come up this far. They say it's all full of poison ivy and things. But I'm not saying that'll happen today."

For several minutes no one spoke. Chester Cricket shifted his weight from one set of legs to the other. "How long *has* it been since anyone was up here?" he asked quietly.

"Well, I guess it's been—it's been almost—over a year," Henry Chipmunk's voice trailed off.

Again there was stillness. In the distance the sound of the human beings laughing over their picnics could be heard. But the silence that gripped the animals was

worse than worrying out loud. "Now let's not get ourselves riled up!" said Harry Cat. "They're all still eating. Just let's let them finish, and then see what happens."

In an hour there could be no doubt: no one was
going to come up to the old cellar. The picnics were
over—except for Jaspar's second dessert; some of the
big kids had already drifted off by themselves, and the
grownups were sitting chatting over their coffee. From
the edge of the orchard the animals stared down, helpless and hopeless.

"And all that work we did," said Henry sadly.

"Not only are those humans stupid—they're lazy!"
said Tucker Mouse. "They should get around more—
go exploring!"

Harry Cat had been watching Jaspar and his family.
He stood up and gave his tail a snap. "Only one thing
left."

"There's nothing left," said Chester.

"Oh yes, there is," said Harry. "Now when I come
back here, I'm going to be running. So everybody get
out of my way!"

"Harry," said Chester anxiously, "what are you going to do?"

"I'm going to pick a fight with Fido."

Before anyone even knew what he meant, the big
cat had darted out from the last row of trees and was
speeding down the hill. Jaspar's family had come across

the log to have their picnic on this side of the brook. They were all sitting on blankets, including Ruff, who was looking at Jaspar expectantly, hoping to get the last of his ice cream. Harry dashed toward them, leaped over a pile of paper plates, and as the Saint Bernard simply stared in amazement—no one had ever picked a fight with *him* before—the cat reared up on his hind legs and took a hefty claw at the dog's tender nose. Then, for good measure, he jumped up in the air, over Ruff's head, and landed, with all claws extended, on his rump. That is what you call adding insult to injury, and Ruff reacted as any self-respecting Saint Bernard would. He let loose a roar of rage and whirled around, scattering paper plates and human beings in every direction. Harry flew off his back and began a mad race toward the orchard. He ran faster than he had ever run in his life—faster even than he thought he could—because he knew that if Ruff ever caught him, there was going to be one cat less in Hedley, Connecticut.

In amazement the animals clustered at the edge of the trees watched all that was happening. It took place so quickly—a minute at most—that they barely had time to tumble aside before Harry flashed past, with Ruff thundering after him. The cat streaked between the two great oak trees—and then pulled his trick. On the very brink of the cellar he swerved aside and darted down the ledge that led to Henry's house. But Ruff knew of no such secret path. He had been up to the ruins of the farm house a few times, sniffing around, but in his present fury he'd forgotten about the great hole that suddenly yawned before him. He tried to brake himself, skidded forward, and then, with a howl of fear now, not anger, he toppled forward, into the cellar.

"Are you all right, Harry?" Tucker Mouse came scrambling breathlessly down the ledge.

"I'm all right," panted Harry. "But you're right— I *am* out of shape. Whee-*oo!* What a chase!" He looked over the edge. "I hope Fido didn't hurt himself." Ruff wasn't hurt. He had landed on a rather large thicket that broke his fall, and he now was searching for a way out of the cellar, yelping for help. "He doesn't sound quite so indignant now, does he?" Harry laughed.

Henry Chipmunk darted up, with Chester Cricket hopping behind him. As soon as they saw that Harry was safe, they joined him and Tucker peering over the ledge. "Let's just hope it takes a lot of people to get him out of there!" said the mouse.

Ruff tried to climb up the tumbled-down west bank of the cellar. But he couldn't make it. The earth there could support the weight of a flock of fieldmice and even a big cat like Harry, but not a Saint Bernard. He kept slipping backward, and his barking grew louder.

"Here they come," whispered Chester.

Hedley Day

On the south bank of the cellar Jaspar and his family appeared. They could tell from the note of fear in his barking that their dog was in trouble, and they followed the sound till they found him. Ellen was with them, but it was her kitty she was worried about. She saw him sitting on the ledge and called him. "I better go over to her," whispered Harry. "Keep your claws crossed." He padded around the rim of the cellar. Ellen picked him up, saw that he wasn't hurt, gave him a kiss on the head, and told him that he was a bad cat for quarreling with Saint Bernards.

"I'll go down and lift him up to you, Dad," said David, Jaspar's brother.

"I'm goin' too!" said Jaspar. Before his mother could say no—which she certainly would have—he was sliding down into the cellar.

David pulled Ruff up the bank as far as he could. Then he grabbed the big dog around the middle and lifted him until his father could reach his front paws. The older man hauled away, managed to roll Ruff over the rim, and got a big sloppy kiss of gratitude. David was pulled up in much the same fashion.

"Jaspar, come out of there this instant!" his mother called.

"I'm comin'," said Jaspar. But he didn't come. He browsed leisurely through the cellar, just seeing what he could see.

"Look at that kid scrounge!" Tucker whispered to

Chester with admiration. "I knew he was a great boy the first day I saw him. Come on, Jaspar! Don't let us down!"

And Jaspar did not let the animals down. He first discovered the Bible, and turned the cover over with interest. But since he was too young to have learned how to read, he didn't realize that it was the family Bible of Joseph He—. Then, on the other side of the rosebush, he saw something else that looked fascinating. With the glee of all great explorers, he held up the sign and called to his parents, "Look what I found!"

"What is it?" said David.

Jaspar crawled up the bank on his hands and knees and handed his brother the sign. "It's mine now!" he said proudly. "I found it."

"Hey, Dad!" David said excitedly. "Look at this!"

David and Jaspar's father examined the sign. "Dear," he called to his wife, "David found a sign down there—and it says Hedley. What do you think that means?"

"*I* found it!" shouted Jaspar. "*I* found it! It's mine." He couldn't climb over the brink of the bank. "Get me outta here!" David pulled him up, and the little boy immediately began whacking his big brother on the chest. "*I* found it!"

"All right, *you* found it!" said David, warding off the blows. "Just stop pounding on me!"

"David," said his father, "run down and tell the others what's happened. This may be important." The boy trotted off through the orchard.

And over in Henry's house a feeling of joy grew thicker and thicker. It lifted the breathless animals up and held them suspended as if in the air. "Well," said Chester Cricket finally, "it's begun!"

Within half an hour the cellar of the old farm house was full of grownups and children, all prowling around discovering things. Many curious old objects were unearthed, and several cases of poison ivy were caught. The grownups all agreed that the Town Council should be notified right away—about the discoveries, not the poison ivy. None of them knew personally any members of the Council, but Nancy's father had a friend who knew the chairman. He took the sign and drove off in his car. An hour later he was back, and with him was the chairman of the Town Council himself.

The chairman was a rather fat man named Veasy. He had to be helped, puffing, down into the cellar. And what he saw there moved him profoundly. It moved him so much that he had to make a speech. After all, it *was* Hedley Day, and the politicians were allowed to make speeches. "Dear friends," he began, "I cannot tell you how touched I am by the discovery of the foundations of the Joseph Hedley homestead! It is a matter of the highest—of the very greatest—"

Tucker's Countryside

Just above Chairman Veasy's head, on the ledge outside Henry's house, the animals were listening to his speech, too. "Here it comes!" whispered Tucker Mouse.

The chairman groped for exactly the right words: "—a matter of the deepest *historical significance!*"

"Didn't I tell you?" squeaked the mouse. "Hic! hic! hic! hic!"

Mr. Veasy went on to say that because of the momentous importance of the discovery, plans to build apartment houses in the Old Meadow would have to be reconsidered. He himself intended to propose, at a special meeting of the Town Council to be called that very night, that the whole area be left just as it was—"as a natural shrine in memory of the great pioneer."

Like all the other boys and girls, Ellen was listening to the chairman's speech as politely as she could. But when she heard those words—about leaving the meadow just as it was—her eyes shone and she had to hold her hands together tight to keep from shouting out loud. When the speech was done, she and Jaspar clapped harder than anyone. (Except for Henry Chipmunk, that is. But he had such tiny hands to clap that none of the humans heard him at all.)

It was truly a marvelous afternoon. The animals watched as the wonderful sign, so fortunately recovered after all these years, was passed from hand to hand. When it came to be Ellen's turn to look at it and hold

it, something about the iron letters struck her as
familiar. Without knowing what she was doing, she
said, "Mother, do you remember that old wooden
sign we used to have in our front yard?"

"Oh, my gosh!" burst out Tucker Mouse. "She's
going to give the whole thing away!"

Mrs. Hadley was standing nearby, chatting with the
other ladies. Jaspar's mother had just been saying how
grand she thought it all was, and just to think—there
they were, standing in the cellar of history! "What,
dear?" Mrs. Hadley said to her daughter. "I'm sorry—
I didn't hear."

"I said, do you remember—" Ellen began. But
abruptly she stopped, looked quickly up at her mother,
and then glanced down at the sign in her hand. A kind
of smile came over her face. "It was nothing, Mother,"
she said. "I forgot what I was going to say." She lowered
the sign behind her back, and as soon as she could,
she passed it on to Jaspar, who kept insisting that it
rightfully was his.

From the ledge above the ladies a sigh of relief so
great went up that it raised a cloud of dust. The dust
settled serenely over the now historic foundations of
the homestead of Joseph Hedley.

All the rest of the day that sly smile lingered on
Ellen's face, the kind of smile you have when you
know a secret. She didn't say a word to anyone, but
she kept wandering off by herself and looking around
the meadow, as if she was searching for someone—

but someone she didn't know. Her mother noticed how strangely she was behaving and asked her if she wasn't happy, now that the Old Meadow had been saved. Ellen said she was very happy, but her happiness, too, was private and quiet, like her smile.

Many other people, including several members of the Town Council, came to inspect the cellar. And they were all just as thrilled—a few gave speeches—as Chairman Veasy had been. It became very crowded around the rim, with the human beings all staring down. When they got the chance, the animals crept off to be by themselves. Harry Cat, too, slipped away from Ellen. He wanted to spend this great afternoon with his friends.

But history, to say nothing of speeches, can become a little tiring. At twilight the people began to leave. When they reached the road, most turned to look back. The meadow looked the same—the hill, the brook, the darkening fields—but somehow now it felt truly important: a "historical" place. They should have known better. The meadow had been important for years, and beautiful, too—and not because of history.

Tucker Mouse, in the meantime, had not been idle. He had done some extensive exploring and scrounging, and what he had found delighted him! "Harry!" he said. "You wouldn't believe it! The whole place is littered with ends of hot dogs, chunks of hamburgers, great gooey gobs of potato salad—!"

"The mind reels!" Harry Cat laughed.

Hedley Day

"I tell you what!" said Chester. "Let's have a party! Goodness knows, we've got something to celebrate! And everybody's invited!"

"Hooray!" came a cry from sundry fieldmice.

"We'll collect all the food and take it down to my stump," said Chester.

"And I want to hear you play," said Tucker. "Some of the human things you learned. Especially that one from the farewell concert you gave in New York."

Henry Chipmunk began jumping up and down. "Let's start right now! All the people have gone."

"Not all of them," said Harry. "Look."

On top of the hill above Simon's Pool, Ellen Hadley was standing. The animals heard her mother call her. "Ellen—it's getting pretty chilly. Don't you think you ought to come in?"

"I will," the girl called back. "In a minute."

"She's been acting funny all afternoon," said Tucker.

"It's that sign," said Chester. "She knows she knows something—but she doesn't know what it is."

Ellen began to walk down the hill, toward her Special Place beside the brook. "Let's see what she's going to do," said Harry. The animals padded and crept and hopped to the thickets surrounding the Special Place.

There was a shiver in the air, a promise of autumn to come, and winter after that. But within the shiver there was also the promise of spring beyond winter, and then the summer, and all the changing, circling seasons that now would be able to come to the meadow. Ellen stood for a moment, looking, listening. Then very softly she said, "I feel sort of silly, talking to no one—but whoever you are—thank you."

She turned, climbed the hill without looking back, crossed the road, and went home.

That night, the night of the day of the Great Discovery, as it came to be known in Hedley, Connecticut, is well remembered by many people.

It is especially well remembered by Mr. Frank Lawler and his wife. Mr. Lawler taught music in one of the Hedley public high schools. On this particular night Mr. Lawler and his wife were driving by the meadow. Just over the bridge where the brook flowed out, Mr. Lawler stopped his car.

"What's wrong?" said his wife.

"Don't you hear that?" said Mr. Lawler.

"Hear what?"

"There's a melody out there in the darkness."

"A *what?*" said Mrs. Lawler.

"It's an insect!" said Mr. Lawler, and his voice began to shake—not from fear. "And it's playing—why, I know that piece! I've heard it on Saturday afternoon, when the Metropolitan Opera is broadcast. It's playing the sextet from *Lucia di Lammermoor!*"

"Dear," said Mrs. Lawler quietly, "if you want to believe that some bug in that meadow knows how to

play opera, I don't mind, Frank. I honestly don't. I love you, dear. But please—let's go home."

In a state of perplexed amazement and pleasure Mr. Lawler started his car and drove off.

But perhaps the person who best remembers the night of the wonderful day is Ellen Hadley. Long after she had gone to bed, she had the feeling that the great events of the afternoon were still not over. Her bedroom faced the meadow, and she kept tiptoeing to the window, to peer out under the blind. Off down to the right, where the willow tree grew, there seemed to be a haze of light: the full moon, she thought, glancing off the brook—and fireflies flickering much later in the season than they should. And often she thought she heard strange sounds—like music at times, and then like clapping, and then like laughter. Could animals laugh, she wondered. Could insects laugh? Could the trees and the brook and even the grass laugh? She didn't know. But whatever the magic of the meadow was, on this special night it was clearly collected beneath the branches of the willow tree, where there was an old stump that the brook curved around. She was almost tempted to put on her clothes and go out in the night and try to see the mystery. But she didn't. It would have made her parents angry. That wasn't the real reason, though. Ellen wisely realized that there are certain kinds of magic which are best left undisturbed.

THIRTEEN

Another Goodbye

Monday morning all the inhabitants of the meadow slept late. Everyone was exhausted from the activity of the past two days, and the party last night had gone on till all hours. It wasn't until noon that Tucker and Chester woke up. They had a quick drink and wash in the brook—it had become Tucker's habit, too, by now —and then headed over to the Hadleys' house, to see what the human beings had decided about the meadow.

At the top of the hill they saw something that struck them both as a very good sign. Frank, the truck driver, had brought back the dirt Bertha had gouged out, and was filling in the hole. And the steam shovel herself was being loaded onto the huge, flat truck that had brought her. Lou was walking backward up a ramp to the truck and was giving Sam directions where to steer Bertha's creeping caterpillar tread. "Steady! Steady!" he called.

"Boy, don't worry about me keepin' ol' Bertha

steady!" Sam called back happily. "It'll sure be more fun to dig some more space for the reservoir than tearin' up this meadow would be!"

Tucker and Chester hurried across the road and around the Hadleys' house to the sun-porch door. Harry Cat, who had gone back after the party, was waiting for them there. "Finally you're here!" he exclaimed, without even so much as a good morning, and began to tell them all the news. "The whole town is buzzing! It's been in the morning newspaper—on the radio—on television! They're calling it a miracle!"

"They should only know how much work went into that 'miracle'!" said Tucker Mouse.

"But what about the meadow?" said Chester.

"Chairman Veasy gets his way," Harry answered. "They're leaving it just the way it is. And they're even going to plant some more trees. The paper said they were going to 'build a natural wilderness.'"

Tucker Mouse shook his head. "Where but Connecticut would you have to 'build a wilderness'!"

"The only thing they're going to add," said Harry, "is a path up to the cellar. So people can go and see it. And Tucker, you'll be very proud to hear that they're going to put up a stone monument with a plaque on it that says: *Site of the Original Joseph Hedley Homestead.*"

"Hm!" sniffed the mouse. "That plaque ought to say, 'Site of the Original Joseph Hedley Homestead—

Another Goodbye

As Invented by Tucker Mouse and Thrown Together Overnight by All the Inhabitants of the Meadow.' "

"And they're changing the name, too," Harry went on. "From now on it's going to be Hedley's Meadow instead of just the Old Meadow. Oh, and look!" Harry held up the front page of the newspaper, which he'd saved to show them. Right in the center of it was a picture of Jaspar, holding the sign. "It says, 'This young boy, who uncovered the sign which proved conclusively that this was the cellar of the Hedley homestead, has generously donated his discovery to the town of Hedley. It will be exhibited, with the Hedley family Bible, in a case under glass in the lobby of the City Hall.' "

"They must have twisted his arm to make him give it up," said Tucker.

Harry laughed. "I heard his mother tell Ellen this morning that he wouldn't let go of it until they promised to put his picture on the front page of the newspaper."

"You wait," said Chester. "He's going to be chairman of the Town Council himself when he grows up!"

"So you see, Chester," said Harry, "you get what you wanted."

"Thanks to Tucker," said Chester Cricket. "And you, too, Harry. If you hadn't trapped Ruff in the cellar, it all would have been in vain."

"But Tucker had the plan," said Harry. He unlatched the door and came out. "Mousiekins—you saved the day!" And he picked Tucker up and gave him a hug.

"Easy, Harry! You wouldn't know your own strength." Harry set the mouse down again. "You know, you can break a person's back from friendship, too."

"And now you've got to help *me*," said Harry. "Because I have a problem."

"What problem?" said Tucker.

"It's Ellen." Harry swished his tail nervously. "She's had me as a pet all summer, but the time's coming when you and I have to think about getting back to New York."

"Don't tell me!" burst out Tucker. "Is the kitty getting sick of all the lobster Newburg and chocolate sundaes?"

"All right, all right—that's enough of that," said Harry. "You've had your share, too."

"You don't have to go right away, do you?" said Chester rather woefully. "I mean—now that the meadow's been saved, we can all enjoy it together."

"Well, not this very day," said Harry. "But pretty soon. I'm beginning to get homesick for neon lights and the rumble of the subway. And the mousiekins here must be worried about his Life Savings."

"My Life Savings—!" Tucker Mouse clutched his chest. "I'd forgotten all about them!"

Another Goodbye

"The day you forget your Life Savings!" said Harry in disbelief.

"No, Harry, I had!" said Tucker. "I've been so busy saving the meadow. I wonder if those nasty rats got everything." He began fidgeting. "Harry, when can we go? When, Harry?"

"When you solve my problem," said the cat. "You've got to find some way so that Ellen won't be unhappy when she loses her pet. Me, that is."

"Hmm." Tucker scratched one ear and wiggled his whiskers. "A very difficult assignment."

"I hope you can't think of anything for a long time," said Chester. "September's beautiful in the meadow."

"So that's it," said Harry. "You come up with a good idea, and then we go back to New York. In the meantime, come over again tomorrow some time. Mrs. Hadley's baking an apple pie for supper, and I'll try to steal you a chunk."

"Apple pie—" A familiar look of glazed rapture came over Tucker's face.

"You know something, Harry," said Chester Cricket. "I think you may be around for quite a while yet."

"I think we may, too!" Harry Cat laughed.

But it wasn't too many days before Tucker Mouse did think of a good idea. August ended and September began. The green, golden summer was flecked here and there with touches of red and brown. School started for Ellen, and this year the little kids, too, were entering the first grade. Tucker and Chester went over to the Hadleys' every day. Harry always had a little delicacy tucked away for his friends. But the mouse knew that however good a cook Mrs. Hadley was, he and Harry couldn't stay in Connecticut forever. So one morning when they were together in the stump, he told Chester his plan.

Chester shook his head and said, "It's wonderful— if he'll do it."

When Harry heard the new idea, he burst out laughing. "He's so timid, though—don't tell him till the very last minute."

For the next two days Harry spent a great deal of time in the meadow. He slept in the stump too, because he wanted Ellen to get used to the notion that he might be getting restless and want to move on. On the third morning, however, when she woke up, there was Harry, sitting on the foot of her bed. "You're back!" she said. "And I thought you were gone for good."

They had breakfast together. Harry's was cat food, but she gave him a little piece of her fried egg, too. The last thing she always did before leaving for school was to pick Harry up and kiss him on the head. When she did so today, Harry licked her hand and gave a long purr. She looked at him curiously. He was such an extraordinary cat! There were times when she felt as if he knew much more about her than she did about him. Harry purred again, and she put him down. He knew it was the last time she would ever see him.

And so, at last, the afternoon came when Tucker and Harry were to leave for New York. All the animals of the meadow wanted them to stay, but they knew how it was when you'd been away from home a long time. At five o'clock, when the light was long and low and lovely, they were all gathered by Simon's Pool to say goodbye, before John Robin guided the cat and the mouse to the station.

"Is she over in her Special Place?" whispered Tucker to Harry.

"Yes. And she's calling me," said Harry. "It makes me feel awful! Hurry up!"

Tucker jumped up on Simon's log. "Dear friends," he began, "before we say goodbye, there is something that still must be taken care of. As most of you know, Harry Cat—who also goes by the name of Kittykitty-kitty—has been living over at the Hadleys' all summer as Ellen's pet. And she has grown to love him. Who could not?—for to know Harry is to love him."

"Hooray!" came a shout from the sundries. It was the first and only time in the history of Connecticut that a crowd of fieldmice had shouted "hooray" for a tomcat.

Tucker continued: "Now, in order that Ellen shouldn't be too unhappy at her tragic loss, we've decided that she ought to have another pet. Nobody can ever replace Harry, but somebody is going to try. And that somebody is—" His right front paw flashed out and pointed straight at— "—*you*, Henry Chipmunk!" He jumped down off the log and patted Henry on the shoulder. "Congratulations, Henry—you are now Ellen Hadley's new pet."

"Me?" the chipmunk asked in a wavering voice. "Why me?" His tiny black nose turned pale.

"I would have volunteered, Henry," said Chester. "But Ellen likes furry folk."

Henry began to stammer. "Well—um—there's a very nice skunk named Joe who lives in the woods beyond the cellar—"

"A very nice skunk named Joe is just what Ellen wouldn't want," said Tucker. "To say nothing of her mother."

"How about Jim Woodchuck?" Henry pleaded. "He's *awfully* good-natured!"

Tucker solemnly shook his head. "My instinct tells me it's you. So don't try to fight your fate, Henry Chipmunk!"

"But—but—whoever heard of a human being having a *chipmunk* for a pet?"

"You can start a new tradition," said Tucker. "Become a pioneer—like me and Joseph Hedley!"

Another Goodbye

"Henry," said Emily, "after all Mr. Mouse has done for us this summer, I think you should do what he wants." When an older sister uses a certain quiet tone of voice, there is nothing much that a younger brother can do.

In a group the animals all marched Henry around the pool and into the thickets surrounding Ellen's Special Place. She was sitting inside the circle of birches, calling Harry and hoping that he would come back. Tucker gave the chipmunk one final encouraging pat on the back. "Go on, Henry. Be a hero."

"I don't know whether I'm going to like living in a human house or not," said Henry doubtfully.

"My guess is, she'll let you live in the meadow, and come and play with you here," said Tucker. "But if worse comes to worst—" He shrugged. "—you'll just have to adjust to hamburgers and chocolate sundaes. Go ahead."

"All right, Mr. Mouse," Henry panted, "I'm going— I really am going—I'm going right now—"

"So go!" commanded Tucker, and pointed at the girl.

Henry scooted into the open, took one flying leap— and landed in Ellen's lap. She was so surprised she almost fell over backwards. Chipmunks were supposed to be shy, elusive creatures, but here this funny little soul was, sitting on his hind legs right in front of her, as if he wanted nothing more in the world than to make friends. Very gently she reached out her fore-finger and stroked his head. And within minutes she had him jumping back and forth over her hand and running around in back of her in a game of hide-and-seek.

"What did I tell you?" said Tucker to Harry. "A perfect match!"

Ellen and Henry played together until it was almost dinnertime. "Will you come back tomorrow?" she said. "I have to go home now." Henry piped "Yes!" in his shrill little voice. She must have understood him too, because she said, "All right, then—you run along home, too!" For the last time she looked around the meadow for her kitty. He was hiding a few feet away, but Ellen couldn't see him. Resigned, and not too unhappy—a cat had his own life to live, she decided—she went home to tell her mother about this marvelous chipmunk that had run out of nowhere to play with her.

The marvelous chipmunk, meanwhile, was breath-lessly describing his adventures to his friends. "Did you see, Mr. Mouse? Did you see? I did it! I did it! I did it! Oh boy oh boy oh boy oh boy!"

"I knew you had it in you, Henry," said Tucker.

The chipmunk giggled, a little embarrassed. "You know—it's kind of nice to be petted!"

"Ah Henry, that's nothing." Harry Cat sighed. "Wait till the first time you have your tummy rubbed!"

Tucker's Countryside

But now it was time for Tucker and Harry to leave, if they were going to catch the evening train to New York. The animals escorted them up the hill, and goodbyes were said all around. Tucker had an especially fond farewell for Beatrice Pheasant. He urged her to keep on with her scrounging and advised her to concentrate on that path the human beings were going to build to the foundations of the Joseph Hedley homestead. People being what people are, he said, there were bound to be a lot of interesting things lost, and why shouldn't she find them as well as anyone else? As for himself, he had Mrs. Hadley's colored glass necklace to add to his collection as a memento of his visit to Connecticut. Last of all, the cat and the mouse said goodbye to their friend Chester Cricket. Like all the partings of friends, this one was both sad and happy.

Just as they were about to go down the hill to the road, Tucker stopped and looked backward. A wreath of mist traced the course of the brook, and the gray autumn twilight lay over the meadow like a magic cloak. "Oh, the countryside!" Tucker Mouse heaved a sigh. "Except for the park in back of the library, this is probably the only countryside I'll ever see."

"Then that's what we ought to call it!" said Chester. "If the human beings can change the Old Meadow's name, so can we! We'll call it Tucker's Countryside! Shall we—?"

All the animals cheered and shouted "Yes!"

Another Goodbye

And that was how the Old Meadow got its second name. Forever after, with its hills and fields and rushing brook, hidden away like a green heart amid all the houses in Connecticut, it was known to the human beings as Hedley's Meadow. But to the animals who lived there it was known as Tucker's Countryside. And of the two groups it would be difficult indeed to say which one enjoyed it and loved it more.

OTHER CAMELOT BOOKS TO ENJOY